"So, Peter . . . um . . . I was wondering," Mandy began, staring at the floor. She was so nervous, she felt as if she were going to faint. "Would you . . . uh . . . like to go with me on Saturday?"

Peter looked confused. "Go where?"

"Oh." Mandy blushed. "Right. Uh . . . I meant, to the Valentine's dance. Whether you would go with me to that." Really smooth, Mandy, she thought miserably.

Mandy was so nervous about Peter's answer, it seemed as if it took him about an hour to say anything. He finally smiled and caught her eye. "Thanks for asking me," he said. "I mean, that's really nice."

Mandy felt her heart leap. He said yes! I can't believe it!

Peter cleared his throat. "But I already have a date." He shrugged just as the bell rang. "I'm really sorry."

Mandy felt her heart plunge right down to her high-top sneakers. "Oh. That's OK," she said quietly.

She turned around and practically ran down the hallway. She had to get out of there as fast as she could. She couldn't let Peter see how upset and embarrassed she was.

No big deal, she kept telling herself as she walked to her locker. It's not that big a deal. But she knew it was. She'd never be able to look Peter in the face again.

Bantam Books in the SWEET VALLEY TWINS AND FRIENDS series.
Ask your bookseller for the books you have missed.

SWEET VALLEY TWINS
AND FRIENDS

Yours For a Day

Written by
Jamie Suzanne

Created by
FRANCINE PASCAL

BANTAM BOOKS
NEW YORK · TORONTO · LONDON · SYDNEY · AUCKLAND

To John Stewart Carmen

RL 4, 008-012

YOURS FOR A DAY
A Bantam Book / February 1994

*Sweet Valley High® and Sweet Valley Twins and Friends® are
registered trademarks of Francine Pascal*

Conceived by Francine Pascal

*Produced by Daniel Weiss Associates, Inc.
33 West 17th Street
New York, NY 10011*

Cover art by James Mathewuse

ISBN: 0-553-48096-0

Published simultaneously in the United States and Canada

*Bantam Books are published by Bantam Books, a division of Bantam
Doubleday Dell Publishing Group, Inc. Its trademark, consisting of the
words "Bantam Books" and the portrayal of a rooster, is Registered in
U.S. Patent and Trademark Office and in other countries. Marca
Registrada. Bantam Books, 1540 Broadway, New York, New York 10036.*

PRINTED IN THE UNITED STATES OF AMERICA

OPM   0 9 8 7 6 5 4 3 2 1

One

◇

"I am not going to ask him!" Mandy Miller cried. "No way. I can't."

It was Thursday morning, and the Unicorn Club, an exclusive group of the most popular girls at Sweet Valley Middle School, had called a special meeting in the art studio at school.

"Come on, it's the only way to find out if he has a date already," Jessica Wakefield argued. "The Valentine's dance is only one week away. If you don't ask him, someone else is going to."

"But he's supposed to ask *her*," Lila Fowler insisted. "She shouldn't have to ask him. That's not how it works."

"There's no law that says the boy has to ask the girl," Mary Wallace pointed out. "If Mandy wants to ask Peter Jeffries to the Valentine's dance, she should."

Mandy shook her head, and her thick reddish-brown hair swung around her shoulders. "You guys don't understand. Whenever I'm around him, I can't say *any*thing. My mind goes completely blank. I mumble. I babble. There's no way I could ask him out."

Mandy wasn't shy at all. But she'd had a crush on Peter for as long as she could remember. They'd actually gone out together once a few months before, although nothing had really come of it. And it seemed as if Peter had gotten even cuter since then. Mandy was usually pretty confident about talking to boys, but around Peter all her confidence vanished. She got all tongue-tied and said idiotic things. The last thing she could do was ask him on a date to one of Sweet Valley Middle School's biggest dances of the year.

"Look, let's get down to business," she told her friends in the Unicorn Club. "We're supposed to be making signs for our fund-raiser."

"What are we calling it?" Jessica pulled the cap off a bright-purple felt-tip marker.

" 'Yours for a Day'?" Ellen Riteman suggested.

"But it's probably going to last two days, remember?" Janet Howell, the Unicorns' president, frowned at her.

"I know, but 'Yours for Two Days' sounds stupid," Ellen said.

"How about 'Buy a Unicorn, Support the Children's Hospital'?" Mary asked.

"Please," Lila said. "I am not going to be *bought* by anybody."

"I know!" Jessica said. "We can advertise it by saying, 'Feel Rich for a Day—Get Your Own Personal Servant!'"

"That's good." Mandy nodded. "I like that."

"I already have about five servants," Lila bragged. "Why do I need another?"

Mandy rolled her eyes. "You don't. This time you're going to *be* one."

Mandy had come up with the idea for the fundraiser the week before, and she was really excited about it. It was going to be based on the auction Sweet Valley High held every year, in which the seniors were auctioned off as servants to the highest bidders. But in this case the Unicorns would be the servants, and the proceeds would go to improving the cancer ward at Children's Hospital.

Mandy had had cancer earlier in the school year. It had been a terrifying experience, but she was fine now. She'd spent several weeks at Children's Hospital, and the doctors and nurses there had been wonderful to her. She'd become good friends with some of the other patients. She desperately wanted to contribute to the hospital in a special way. And so far all the Unicorns wanted to help her.

"Maybe we should ask the whole school to participate in this," Lila said. "We'd raise a lot more money."

"And that way some people could be masters, and some servants," Janet said. "Right?"

"That's a great idea," Mandy said excitedly. "Maybe we should make it more like a lottery than an auction. We can have two lists—masters and servants—and then we can match up people in a random drawing. That way we can get everyone involved."

"Random?" Jessica said. "But you know what that means. We could get stuck with someone really bad."

"Or really good," Mary said, winking at Mandy. "Like Peter Jeffries, for instance."

"Right," Jessica said. "And then it would be the perfect opportunity to ask him to the—"

"Stop!" Mandy cried.

"I can't believe how badly you guys lost yesterday," Todd Wilkins said at lunchtime in the cafeteria. "I mean, I know you haven't played a lot of tennis, but you didn't even win one game off us."

Elizabeth Wakefield glanced at her best friend, Amy Sutton, and frowned. Todd and Ken Matthews had been teasing them all morning, and she was getting pretty sick of it. "You're the guy who took tennis lessons all last summer," she said to Todd.

"Yeah, but you guys are usually really good at sports," Ken said. "I guess tennis just isn't your game." He shrugged and took a bite of vanilla pudding.

"If you guys want a rematch, we'll be ready anytime," Amy declared.

Ken shook his head. "Too easy."

"Yeah, we like to be challenged when we play," Todd teased.

Elizabeth groaned. She couldn't believe what macho jerks they were being.

"Hey, look!" Ken said, standing up. "Charlie and Jerry are arm wrestling." He pointed to a table across the lunchroom.

"Cool! Let's go check it out." Todd jumped up, and the two of them walked over to the other side of the cafeteria, where a crowd was forming.

"Give me a break," Amy complained. "Everyone's getting romantic about the Valentine's dance next weekend, and all Ken and Todd are interested in is arm wrestling and beating us at tennis."

"I know," Elizabeth said. "They're being so obnoxious! Let's make sure we really crush them next time."

"If we don't, we'll never hear the end of it," Amy muttered.

Elizabeth took the bread off her BLT sandwich and dipped her knife into the small bowl of mayonnaise on the table. She stopped and examined the knife. "Wait a sec—this is the mayonnaise, right?"

"I think so," Amy said. "It does look exactly like the vanilla pudding, doesn't it?"

Elizabeth put a tiny amount on her finger and tasted it. "Yeah, this is the mayo." She started spreading some on the bread. "Can you imagine putting pudding on a sandwich?"

Amy looked at the bowls of pudding on Ken's and Todd's trays. "Eating a spoonful of mayonnaise when you thought it was pudding would be even worse."

Elizabeth smiled. "Are you thinking what I'm thinking?"

Amy waggled her eyebrows. "Maybe we can't beat them at tennis, but we *can* get them back for being such jerks," she said. She glanced across the cafeteria, where Ken and Todd were still cheering on the arm-wrestling match.

Elizabeth quickly smoothed over one of the mayonnaise bowls and put it on Todd's tray, replacing his uneaten bowl of pudding. Amy scooped some mayonnaise out of the other small bowl, so that it looked just like Ken's half-eaten bowl of pudding. They had just finished and were giggling mischievously when the boys came walking back toward the table.

"Who won?" Elizabeth asked, trying to sound casual.

"Charlie," Todd said, sliding into his chair. "He always does."

"Mmmm." Amy licked her spoon and set it down on her tray. "The pudding's great."

Elizabeth kicked her under the table. She was trying as hard as she could not to start laughing.

"It is pretty decent," Ken said. He dug his spoon into the bowl and took a large bite just as Todd did the same thing.

It took them several seconds to react.

"Aaaaaagh!" Ken cried, jumping up. He put a napkin over his mouth.

"Foul! What is that?" Todd shouted. He had such a sick expression on his face, he looked almost green.

Elizabeth and Amy both dissolved into laughter.

"Mmmmm. Mayonnaise," Elizabeth choked out.

Todd and Ken glared at them angrily.

"Oh, come on," Amy said, trying to catch her breath. "Where's your sense of humor?"

"Don't get mad," Elizabeth said.

Ken glanced at Todd.

"Yeah, get even," the boys said at exactly the same time.

"Archie, leave me alone," Mandy told her nine-year-old brother on Friday afternoon. "I need to make a phone call."

"So do I," Archie said, folding his arms across

his chest. "It's an emergency. I need to ask Dylan if he has my Don Mattingly card."

"Gee, Archie. Why not just call nine-one-one?" Mandy asked, rolling her eyes.

"Very funny."

"Listen, I'll let you know when I'm done, OK?" Mandy said.

She had finally gotten up her nerve to call Peter Jeffries, and she didn't want to put it off any longer. If she had to wait while Archie blabbed about baseball cards for twenty minutes, she'd definitely lose her nerve.

"OK, but hurry," Archie said, frowning. Then he ran upstairs.

Mandy picked up the telephone on the living-room table. What was so hard about asking someone to a dance? She'd never had a hard time talking to a boy before. She never had trouble talking to anyone. So why was she feeling so shy now?

Maybe it was because Peter was perfect. OK, so nobody was perfect, but Peter came pretty close. He was a fantastic football player, he was great at math, and he was really funny, too. She loved the way his dark brown hair curled at the back of his neck, and how blue his eyes were. That was what made it so impossible for her to talk to him.

But if there was one thing Mandy had learned from being sick, it was not to waste time. There was no sense sitting around waiting for something to happen, when you could do something about it. Mandy wasn't going to wait for Peter to ask her. Mary and Jessica were right—there was nothing wrong with a girl asking a boy out.

She flipped through the phone book until she found the Jeffrieses' number. Then, before she could think about it anymore, she dialed.

While the phone rang, she quickly rehearsed her line. *Hello, may I please speak with Peter? Oh, hi, Peter. It's Mandy Miller. I was wondering, would you like to go to the Valentine's dance with me next Saturday?*

She was startled when someone actually answered.

"Hello?"

It was Peter!

Mandy was so flustered, she hung up the phone as fast as she could.

What's my problem? Why can't I just ask him, like a normal person?

"What are you going to do this weekend?" Elizabeth asked Amy as they walked down the hall to their lockers after school on Friday. "Do you have any plans?"

"Not really," Amy said.

Elizabeth was feeling much better now that she and Amy had apologized to Ken and Todd, and

Ken and Todd had apologized for rubbing in the tennis game. They'd all laughed about it and called a truce.

Elizabeth smiled as she saw Winston Egbert walking toward them. "Hi, Winston," she said.

"What's up?" Amy asked him.

Winston stopped and bowed in front of them. Then, from behind his back, he produced an envelope with a dramatic flourish. "For you, mademoiselles."

"What is it?" Amy took the envelope from him and looked at it suspiciously.

"It is zee secret surprise, from two young gentlemen you are perhaps acquainted with, yes?" Winston said in a phony French accent. "Have a *beaucoup* nice day." Then he bowed again and walked off.

"Open it," Elizabeth urged Amy. It had to be something from Ken and Todd.

"Maybe they're finally inviting us to the Valentine's dance," Amy said eagerly, tearing open the envelope. She pulled out a sheet of paper with some kind of drawing on it.

"What is it?" Elizabeth peered over Amy's shoulder.

"It's a map," Amy said, looking puzzled. " 'Follow me and you will see who your Valentines will be,' " she read out loud. "Isn't that cute?"

"Look, instead of an X to mark the spot, there's a heart," Elizabeth pointed out.

"Oh, this is sooo romantic," Amy said, sighing.

"Cut it out!" Elizabeth said, laughing. "You're getting all mushy on me. Come on, let's figure out where we're supposed to go."

They studied the map for a few seconds.

"OK, we're supposed to start at the lunchroom," Amy said. They walked back to the lunchroom, then followed the map's arrows upstairs past their classrooms, down a flight of steps to the library, and past the gymnasium. "Why are they making us walk this whole way?" Amy wondered.

"This is fun," Elizabeth said. "I love treasure hunts."

"OK. We're in the right place," Amy said a minute later, when they walked into their math classroom.

"Look! There's something stuck to the blackboard," Elizabeth said.

They hurried over, and Amy peeled off the envelope taped to the board. "'You're almost there, just close the door, and you'll find what you're looking for on the floor,'" she read.

Amy and Elizabeth turned from the board and went over to the door. "They must be behind it," Elizabeth whispered.

She pushed the door shut, and Amy bent over to pick up a piece of paper on the floor.

Suddenly, a torrent of cold water cascaded

down, completely drenching them.

"Arrrrrgh!" Elizabeth cried as water streamed down her back.

"What is this?" Amy yelled, blinking through the water in her eyes.

Elizabeth looked at the top of the door, where a huge bucket hung dangling from a rope. "I can't believe it. Todd and Ken rigged this whole thing up just to get us!" Elizabeth tried to wipe the water off her face with her shirtsleeve, which was also soaked.

Amy unfolded the wet piece of paper she'd picked up. "Don't be a wet blanket—come to the dance with us," it said. "Signed, Todd and Ken."

"Ha ha," Elizabeth muttered, pushing her wet hair back. "Very funny."

"Unbelievable!" Amy said angrily, wringing out her wet cotton sweater. "I mean, we called a truce. They said they weren't mad anymore!"

"You know what this means?" Elizabeth asked Amy.

"We're not going to the dance with them?" Amy said.

"No," Elizabeth said, squeezing water out of her long blond hair. "This means *war*."

"You're kidding," Jessica said, laughing. "What jerks!"

"I know." Elizabeth took a bite of an apple.

Jessica and Elizabeth were hanging out together on Friday night, getting ready to watch a horror movie they'd rented.

"Aaron would never do something like that to *me*," Jessica said.

Of course, Jessica wasn't surprised that Todd and Ken had pulled such a stupid stunt. They could be so immature sometimes. She was glad Todd was Elizabeth's boyfriend and not hers. But then, she and Elizabeth did most things differently. Even though they were twins, with identical long, sun-streaked blond hair and blue-green eyes, they were about as different as two twelve-year-olds could be.

Jessica spent most of her time with her friends in the Unicorn Club, which was the coolest club at school. She was best friends with Lila Fowler, who was the complete opposite of Elizabeth's best friend, Amy Sutton. Lila was pretty and rich, and she loved shopping even more than Jessica. Amy was a tomboy who liked playing softball more than mall crawling.

Elizabeth loved to write, and she worked on the official sixth-grade newspaper, the *Sweet Valley Sixers*. And she took her schoolwork very seriously. Jessica didn't. Her favorite part of school was hanging out with her friends and cheering with the Booster Club at all the football and basketball games. But even though the twins had totally different interests, they managed to stay very close.

"Yeah, well, Amy and I are going to get them back somehow," Elizabeth vowed.

"You'd better," Jessica said. She grinned at Elizabeth. "Hey, did you see the signs we put up for the 'Rich for a Day' thing the Unicorns are doing?"

"No. What is it?" Elizabeth asked.

Jessica quickly explained the Unicorns' plans for the lottery to raise money for the Children's Hospital. "We asked Mr. Clark for permission, and he said we could sign people up on Monday, during lunch," she said. "Then people will be servants or masters on Thursday and Friday."

"That sounds like fun," Elizabeth said. "I'm impressed with you all. The Unicorns are actually doing some good."

Jessica glared at her. "Lizzie! Thanks a lot."

Elizabeth laughed. "Just kidding. Sort of. Anyway, I'll definitely sign up."

"Good. Because the more people that sign up, the more fun it's going to be," Jessica said. "Besides, we'll raise a lot of money, too."

"So which are you going to be, master or servant?" Elizabeth asked.

"Both," Jessica said. "As long as I don't draw Lila's name, I'm not worried. Lila's going to make some poor person's life miserable!"

Two

"Sign up now!" Jessica called to the people in the lunch line on Monday at noon. "Help Children's Hospital!"

"What do we have to do?" Bruce Patman asked, stopping by the table that Jessica and Janet had set up in the middle of the lunchroom.

"Just sign here," Jessica told him, giving him a big smile.

Bruce frowned. "I don't sign anything until I know what it is."

"OK, OK. It's called Feel Rich for a Day," Jessica started to explain.

"Like I don't know what that feels like," Bruce scoffed, and a few of his friends laughed. Bruce's family was one of the wealthiest in Sweet Valley.

"Anyway," Jessica continued, "for no money at

all you can volunteer to be someone's servant either Thursday or Friday. For five dollars you can be someone's boss for one day, and for ten dollars you can be someone's boss for two days."

"Volunteer to be someone's servant? Who thought up this stupid idea?" Charlie Cashman asked.

Janet Howell cleared her throat. "It's not a stupid idea, and it's for a good cause. The hospital's trying to build a new cancer ward. Besides, don't you know they do this kind of thing at high school all the time?" She sighed, as if she were completely exasperated with them.

"Well, um, OK," Charlie said with a smile. "Can I borrow a pen?"

Jessica smiled. It helped to have one of the prettiest and most popular girls in school sitting next to her. Janet was an eighth-grader, and half the boys in school had a crush on her.

"Put me on the list of bosses," Bruce said, pulling out his wallet.

"Do it yourself," Janet retorted, handing him a pen.

Jessica was calmly counting up the number of signatures they already had when she had an eerie feeling that someone was watching her. She looked up. Lloyd Benson was staring at her through hist-thick black-framed glasses.

"What now, Jessica?" Lloyd asked, pushing his glasses up on his nose. "Are you predicting the next occurrence of a hurricane this time? Or maybe a tornado?"

Jessica sighed. A few weeks before, she had been convinced she could predict earthquakes, and Lloyd, the king of all nerds, had followed Jessica around constantly, treating her like a science experiment. Jessica didn't feel like being reminded of the experience. "No, Lloyd, I'm not," she said.

Lloyd set his briefcase on the floor. "So what's this for?"

"Nothing you'd be interested in," Jessica said.

Mandy kicked Jessica's leg under the table. "We need as many people as possible," she hissed. "It's not going to ruin anything if he signs up."

Jessica wasn't so sure she agreed, but she decided Lloyd's money was as good as anyone else's. Just as long as *she* didn't end up with him. "We're raising money for Children's Hospital. You should sign up," she told Lloyd, offering him a pen. "It's only five dollars for one day, or ten dollars for two, or you can participate for free by volunteering to be a servant one day. A lot of us are volunteering to be a servant and paying to be a master, too."

"Do the profits really go to the hospital?" Lloyd asked.

"Of course!" Jessica said. "What do you think, *we're* going to keep it?"

"You're not exactly trustworthy," Lloyd said, "in my experience."

"Ask someone else if you don't believe me," Jessica said. "Mandy, this is for real, isn't it?"

Mandy nodded. "Some of our parents are donating money, too, to match whatever we get. We want to give the hospital at least five hundred dollars."

"Hmmm. Well, OK." Lloyd pulled a mechanical pencil out of his plastic pocket protector and added his name to the "masters" list. "Of course, the mathematical chances that I'll end up with a servant I can actually work with are quite slim."

"You can say that again," Mandy said, laughing with Jessica as Lloyd walked away.

"What did you say to Ken when you saw him?" Elizabeth asked Amy at lunch.

"Nothing. I'm not talking to him," Amy declared.

"Wait a minute," Julie Porter said, putting down her turkey sandwich. "I thought you guys were going to the dance together on Saturday."

"Not the way things are going now," Amy grumbled.

"You're kidding," Julie said. "Because of the joke they played on you Friday?"

"Yeah, and because they've been acting like jerks for the past week," Elizabeth said. "They haven't even really asked us to go yet, unless you count that soaked piece of paper telling us not to be wet blankets."

"I bet they thought they were being really smart," Amy said. "They got our hopes up, and then—wham!"

"Look. There they are now," Julie said. "Signing up for the master-servant lottery." She pointed to the table where Jessica and the other Unicorns were sitting.

"Whoever gets either of them for a master will be sorry," Elizabeth said, watching Todd across the room. "They'll probably make their servants throw pies at us, or booby-trap our lockers."

"No, they'll make whoever it is clean their rooms or empty out their stinky gym lockers or something," Amy said.

"Look out—here they come," Julie warned.

Elizabeth pretended to be examining the contents of her lunch bag when Todd and Ken walked up.

"So what's going on?" Ken said casually, taking a seat beside Amy.

Amy didn't say anything.

"Hi, Elizabeth. What's up?" Todd asked.

Silence. Elizabeth took a bite of butterscotch pudding and ignored him.

"You guys aren't still mad at us, are you?" Ken asked.

"You're not holding a grudge just because of

that little joke we played, are you?" Todd asked.

"Little joke?" Amy said. "You call a bucket of ice water over our heads a little joke?"

Ken laughed. "We saw you guys leave—we were hiding in the next classroom. You were pretty soaked. It was so funny."

Amy glared at him. "Just hilarious," she said flatly. She glanced around the table. "Don't you have somewhere else you could sit?"

"Come on, guys. Don't be mad at us. Look, I'm sorry," Todd said. "Really."

"Yeah, me too," Ken added. "I guess we went a little too far with that one."

"Please forgive us?" Todd asked.

"Yeah. Where's your sense of humor?"

Elizabeth shrugged. "OK, OK."

"Fine," Amy said. "But don't do anything like that again, or you're dead."

"So did you guys sign up for the Unicorns' fund-raiser?" Elizabeth asked.

"Yeah, who are you going to torture?" Amy asked.

"Nobody," Todd said.

"There weren't many people who signed up to be servants, so we agreed to do that instead," Ken said. "It's a lot cheaper, and Jessica practically begged us."

"So you're going to be servants?" Elizabeth asked. "That should be fun." She glanced across the table at Amy and smiled. She had a feeling

Amy was thinking the same thing she was.

Getting Todd and Ken as servants would be the best revenge ever.

"And it's for a really good cause," Mandy told Jim Sturbridge. "All the money's going to the hospital, to help build the new cancer ward."

"OK. I'll do it," Jim said.

"Master or servant?" Mandy asked. "Actually, if you could volunteer to be a servant, that would be great. We need more of them."

"Well . . . I guess for one day it would be all right." Jim added his name to the list.

"Thanks a lot," Mandy said, smiling at him. After Jim left, she started scanning the lists. They needed a few more servants, and then there would be enough to make matches with each master. She was impressed with the number of people who'd signed up. The fund-raiser was going to be even more successful than she'd hoped.

"Hey, Mandy. What's going on?"

Mandy looked up. She couldn't believe it. Peter Jeffries was standing right in front of her. She was about to open her mouth, but she froze when she remembered how she'd tried to call him over the weekend. *He probably knows it was me*, she thought in a panic. She took a deep breath and tried to calm herself down. *Mandy, get a grip—don't be ridiculous.*

Just answer him like a normal human being.

"Oh, um . . . it's for charity," Mandy said, blushing. "For . . . um . . . Children's Hospital."

Peter looked confused. "What's for Children's Hospital?"

"This . . . this, uh . . . mister—I mean master and servant . . . uh . . . thing," Mandy explained. *I sound so stupid! I'm the one who organized the whole thing, and I sound like a complete airhead.* "It costs ten dollars for one day or five dollars for two."

Peter raised his eyebrows. "It's cheaper for two days?"

"Oh, right . . . uh . . . it's the other way around," Mandy said, feeling flustered. "Or you can volunteer to be a servant. And the money goes to help the hospital."

"That's cool," Peter said, nodding. "I'd like to help out."

"So would you like to sign up?" Mandy asked timidly.

"Sure," Peter said.

Mandy handed him a pen, praying he didn't notice how much her hand was shaking.

He took it from her. "I think I'll be a servant. It seems like that listiis kind of short," Peter said.

Mandy watched him write down his name and smiled. *I knew he was a nice guy,* she thought.

"Thanks a lot," she said when he turned to go.

"See you," Peter said, smiling at Mandy.

She watched him walk across the lunchroom and out the door.

"So did you ask him to the dance?"

Mandy looked up, startled. Jessica was standing there with a plate of chocolate-chip cookies.

"Are you kidding?" Mandy shook her head. "I could barely breathe." She let out a loud sigh.

"Mandy! That was the perfect opportunity!" Jessica said.

"I know, I know," Mandy groaned. "But I can't even put full sentences together when he's around. I tried to explain the master-servant thing, and I babbled. I made no sense. You should have heard me. And look at my hands!"

"Don't worry about it," Jessica said. "He probably didn't even notice. But there are only five days until the dance. So you'd better ask him soon, before he gets another date."

Mandy just shook her head. She knew, deep down inside, that she could never ask Peter to the dance. There was just no way. Even if she could bring herself to ask him, which she obviously couldn't, the thought of his saying no was just too terrible to risk.

Jessica glanced at the list of people who'd signed up. "Hey, who knows—maybe you'll get to be his boss for a day. Then you can order him to go to the dance with you!" She laughed.

"Oh, *that* sounds romantic," Mandy said, shaking her head and laughing too.

"Elizabeth, this is the perfect opportunity," Amy urged. "If we can get to be Todd's and Ken's bosses, we can *really* win the war."

"The war?" Elizabeth asked, looking up from her desk in the *Sweet Valley Sixers* office. It was Tuesday afternoon, and she was finishing up an article on the Unicorns' fund-raiser for the newspaper.

"Remember? You said it was a war," Amy said, sitting on the edge of the desk.

"I know. But they *were* being pretty nice today," Elizabeth said. "They did apologize and everything."

"What a wimp," Amy said, laughing. "I can't believe you're going to forgive them that easily. Remember walking home with wet hair, wet clothes, and wet squishy shoes?" she asked.

"Yeah," Elizabeth said, tapping her pencil against the desk. "You're right. We can't let them off that easily. But what are we going to do?"

Amy drummed her fingers on the table. "How are they going to match up people to be masters and servants?" she asked. "Did Jessica explain it when you interviewed her for the article?"

"It's a random drawing, as far as I know,"

Elizabeth said. "They're going to put everybody's name in a hat or something."

Amy hopped off the desk and started pacing around the office. "Then we'll just have to make it *un*random."

"What?" Elizabeth asked. "How?"

"Jessica's going to be involved, right? And she is your sister," Amy said.

"Right. . . . So what are you saying? You want me to ask her to match us up with Ken and Todd?" Elizabeth asked.

"Exactly," Amy said with a smile. "Then we'll be able to torture them as much as we want."

"But . . . that's cheating," Elizabeth said.

"Exactly," Amy repeated.

Elizabeth thought about it for a second. She wasn't exactly the cheating type. Amy flashed her a mischievous grin, and she couldn't help smiling back.

"OK, I'll do it," she told Amy.

Amy smacked her hand on the table. "This is going to be fun!"

Three

"Jessica, I need to ask you a big favor." Elizabeth walked into her sister's bedroom Tuesday night and sat on her bed. "Really big."

"You want me to lend you my new purple dress for the Valentine's dance," Jessica said. "I can't—I'm going to wear it."

"No. It's bigger than that," Elizabeth said. She took a deep breath. "Amy and I came up with a great way of getting back at Todd and Ken, but we need your help."

"Of course I'll help," Jessica said. "What do you want me to do? Pretend to be you?"

Elizabeth shook her head. "No, what I want to ask you is bigger than that."

Jessica rubbed her hands together. "This sounds good—tell me!"

"Well, I was wondering if you could arrange it so that Amy and I get to have Ken and Todd as our servants in the drawing tomorrow," Elizabeth said.

"What do you mean?" Jessica asked.

"Instead of it being a random drawing, is there some way you could make sure we get them? You know, could you cheat for me?" Elizabeth asked.

"*What?* My sister wants to cheat?" Jessica gasped and fell to the floor, pretending to faint.

Elizabeth laughed. She knew she was usually the one who tried to talk Jessica *out* of doing things like this. "It's for a good cause. Amy and I have to get them back. We thought if they were our servants, then we could make them do all kinds of incredibly embarrassing things."

"Like what?" Jessica asked.

"You'll see," Elizabeth said. She wanted to keep her and Amy's plans a secret. "So what do you think? Will you do it? Please?"

"Yeah, OK. I can't wait to see this. But," Jessica said, "you owe me one."

"OK," Elizabeth said. "Whatever you want."

"Is everyone ready?" Jessica stood with her hand poised above the trash can full of little index cards with people's names on them. She looked out across the cafeteria.

It was Wednesday, at the beginning of lunch

period in the cafeteria, and a big crowd of students had gathered around the table where Jessica and the other Unicorns were holding the master-servant drawing. Jessica smiled at the crowd. She loved being the center of attention.

"Hurry up!" Bruce yelled. "We don't have all day!"

"Yeah, some of us want to eat sometime before dinner," Ken added.

"Just be patient, everybody!" Jessica tossed her hair over her shoulder, then started rummaging in the trash can to find the cards she wanted. She had stuck little blue dot stickers all over Ken's and Todd's cards so she could feel them, and slipped them in when none of the other Unicorns were looking. Todd's had three dot stickers and Ken's had six. "First I'm going to pick for . . . Elizabeth."

"No fair!" Jim yelled.

"She signed up first, and we're going in order," Jessica told him. "Elizabeth's servant will be . . ." She pulled out an index card. She waited a second before readingtthe name on it, so it wouldn't look as if she instantly recognized it. "Todd Wilkins!"

"Is this thing rigged?" Winston asked.

"Next I'm drawing for Amy Sutton," Jessica announced. She picked out the next card and studied it for a brief second. "Her servant will be Ken Matthews! Wow, what a coincidence."

There were grumbles in the crowd. "Let someone else pick! This thing's fixed!" Bruce yelled.

Jessica shrugged and handed the trash can to Mandy, who was next to her. Now that she'd accomplished what she wanted, she didn't care who did the drawing.

"I'm going to draw for Jessica, because she's next on the list," Mandy said. "Jessica's servant will be—" She stared at the card. "Me?"

Jessica grinned. She was glad she had Mandy as her servant. She probably wouldn't make her do much of anything, but it would be fun anyway. And Mandy was much better than somebody like . . . well, Lloyd Benson, for example.

"I'll pick next," Lila declared loudly above the grumbling in the crowd. "The next person on the master list is . . . Lloyd Benson."

Jessica couldn't help grinning. Whoever got stuck being Lloyd's servant was going to be miserable. She could just picture him, making his servant participate in science experiments or play computer chess with him.

Lila put her hand in the trash can and mixed all the index cards around. "OK, here we go." She grabbed a card and pulled it out. When she read it, she burst out laughing.

"I wonder who it is," Mandy said softly to Jessica.

"I don't know, but it must be someone good," Jessica replied.

"Lloyd, are you here?" Lila called.

"Present," Lloyd said, making his way up to the table. "May I please have the name of my assistant?"

"Sure," Lila said, grinning. "Your servant for the next two days is . . . Jessica Wakefield!"

Jessica sank down in her chair. *No way! Of all the rotten luck. I should have cheated for myself instead of for Elizabeth!* Jessica thought miserably.

Mandy couldn't believe how well the drawing was going. Except for a few bad matches, like Jessica and Lloyd, everyone seemed pretty happy with the way things were turning out. She, like a lot of other people, had signed up to be both a master and a servant. Now that she knew she'd lucked out in the master department, she was waiting nervously to see who she would get as a servant. So far Peter's card hadn't been picked, and she knew her name was getting close on the list of masters.

"Belinda's servant will be . . . Elizabeth Wakefield!" Janet announced. "And next on the master list is Aaron Dallas. His servant will be . . . Grace Oliver!"

"I'm next," Lila said to Janet, pointing at the list. "Pick someone good."

Mandy smiled. *She* wouldn't want to be Lila's servant, and she and Lila were pretty good friends. Lila had a lot of experience ordering people around.

"Lila Fowler's servant is . . . Peter Jeffries," Janet

said. She gave Mandy a sympathetic glance. "Sorry," she said under her breath.

Mandy felt her heart sink. She was disappointed—but a little relieved, too.

"I wish you'd gotten Peter," Lila whispered. "Maybe we can switch."

"No, that's OK," Mandy said. "It's better this way, actually." Now she wouldn't have to worry about what she'd say to Peter, or how she'd act when she was with him. She was off the hook.

Janet handed the trash can to Lila. "Your turn. My name's coming up, and I can't draw for myself."

"There aren't too many people left," Mandy said to Janet, sitting down next to her.

"Mandy Miller's servant will be . . . Jim Sturbridge," Lila said.

Mandy glanced at Jim and smiled. Jim was a pretty nice guy. She wouldn't mind hanging out with him.

"And now, for our last name on the master list, Winston Egbert," Lila said in a dramatic voice. "Let me see." She reached into the can and pulled out the lavt card.

"Who hasn't been drawn yet?" Mandy wondered.

"You mean, who's going to get stuck with Winston? I don't know," Janet said. "I can't—wait a second—"

Lila grinned. "Winston, I am *very* pleased to announce that your servant will be Miss Janet Howell."

"Ugh," Janet groaned.

Winston walked over to Janet and looked down his nose at her. "Do you have any references?"

"References?" Janet replied. "What are you talking about?"

"I want to know if you're qualified to be my servant," Winston said in a snooty voice, trying not to laugh. "Would you please give me a copy of your résumé?"

Janet narrowed her eyes and glared at him. "Would you please disappear?"

"So that was pretty lucky, huh?" Todd asked. "I'm glad I'm working for you, instead of Lila or Janet or someone like that."

Elizabeth couldn't help smiling. "Yep. It's your lucky day."

"I can't believe our names got picked first," Ken said. "It's pretty incredible."

"Talk about coincidences," Amy agreed, nodding. "It's like it was meant to be or something." She nudged Elizabeth's foot under the table.

"So now we'll have to think of some things for you guys to do." Elizabeth tapped her fork against her plate. "This is going to be hard."

"You're going to let us off easy, aren't you?" Ken asked.

"Sure," Amy said, nodding.

"Yeah, we wouldn't want to take advantage of you or anything," Elizabeth added.

"Well, I'm going to grab a glass of water," Todd said, getting up from his chair.

"I'll come with you," Ken said. "I need more cookies. You guys want anything?"

"No thanks," Amy said. "We'll wait until tomorrow to start ordering you around."

Elizabeth could hardly wait until Ken and Todd were out of earshot before she started laughing. "This is going to be great!"

"I know," Amy said. "I can't wait until tomorrow."

"So what should their first task be?" Elizabeth asked.

"Let's make a list." Amy grabbed a napkin and a pen. "OK, first of all, let's talk . . . severe discomfort."

"And don't forget public humiliation," Elizabeth said. "There's going to be a lot of that."

"You're not eating, Jessica," Ellen said. "What's wrong?"

Jessica shook her head unhappily. "Why couldn't I have been Aaron's servant instead of Lloyd's?" she complained. "It wouldn't even have to be Aaron. *Anyone* except Lloyd would be great."

"How about me? I got stuck with Winston," Janet said. "This is going to be pure torture. It's bad enough to be a servant, but a *nerd's* servant? Maybe I'll stay home sick tomorrow."

"Come on, you guys, it's not that terrible," Mandy said. "It's only for one day."

"Easy for you to say. You got Jim," Janet muttered. "We got two geekbrains."

Jessica looked at Lloyd, who was sitting a few tables away. He seemed to be reading some kind of science textbook.

"Look, Mandy, there's Peter." Mary pointed to him. He was headed toward their table.

"He's coming this way," Lila said. "Maybe he's going to ask you to the dance."

"I doubt it," Mandy said. She nervously arranged and rearranged everything on her tray. Jessica had never seen her friend look so flustered before.

Peter stopped in front of their table. "Hi, Mandy," he said. "I have a question."

Mandy looked up and smiled, her face turning bright pink. "Sure. Go ahead."

"What time does this thing start tomorrow?" Peter asked. "When we get to school?"

Mandy's smile faded. "Oh, um, I don't know. I mean, I haven't thought about that yet. What do you guys think?" she asked the other Unicorns.

"I think it should start at school," Jessica said. *The less time it lasts, the better.*

"Yeah, I agree," Janet said.

"OK, then that's when it starts," Mandy told Peter. "Is that OK with you?"

"No problem," Peter said. He turned to Lila. "See you tomorrow, Lila. I mean, boss." He smiled, then turned to walk away.

"Rats! I thought he was going to ask you out," Jessica said. "I bet he was, and then he lost his nerve when he got over here."

"I don't think so," Mandy said. "I don't think he likes me. Anyway, if he wanted to ask me to the dance, he would have done it already. It's not like he hasn't had time."

Jessica frowned. She hated seeing her friend so miserable. There had to be *some*thing she could do to get Mandy and Peter together.

Four

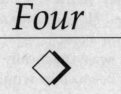

Wednesday night Jessica was lying in bed, trying to fall asleep. But she couldn't. She kept thinking about what she should ask Mandy to do for her the next day. She was going to have her very own servant. She didn't want to waste the opportunity.

She pictured Mandy following her around, opening doors for her, carrying her books. Then, after school, they could go to the mall, and she could tell Mandy to buy her that purple sweatshirt she'd been wanting for the past month.

I guess I can't do that, Jessica thought, turning over and punching up her pillow. *We didn't say anything about servants paying for things.*

She didn't want to be obnoxious. It would be one thing if she had Lila as her servant. It would be a lot of fun to torture Lila. But Mandy was too nice for that. Mandy was one of the coolest, nicest people Jessica knew.

She thought back to how disappointed Mandy looked at the lunch table that day. What was the matter with Peter Jeffries? Couldn't he see how great Mandy was? *He must have rocks in his head if he doesn't ask her to the dance.*

Poor Mandy was practically suffering from a broken heart, all because he wouldn't ask her to the dance, and she wasn't brave enough to ask him. It was like something out of an old romantic movie. If only there was some way to get them together . . .

Suddenly Jessica shot up in her bed. "I've got it!" she said out loud. There was a way to get them together—and she was it. She'd order Mandy to ask Peter to the dance! She'd be helping them both out. She'd be aiding the course of true love. Jessica snuggled back under the covers. She couldn't wait for tomorrow. Mandy was going to be so happy!

"Hello, may I speak with Jessica Wakefield, please?"

Jessica cradled the phone on her shoulder and set her plate on the counter. It was Thursday morning, and she was just finishing her breakfast. *Why does this voice sound so familiar?* she wondered.

"This is Jessica," she said. "Who's this?"

"This is Lloyd Benson. I'm your boss today, if you recall," Lloyd said.

Ugh. "I recall," Jessica said out loud. *Do I ever.* "But, Lloyd—"

"As your first duty I'd like to ask you to pick up some doughnuts for me on the way to school," Lloyd continued, interrupting her. "There's a Daylight Doughnuts Shop in your neighborhood, isn't there?"

"But, Lloyd, the master-servant stuff doesn't start until we get to school."

"It didn't say that anywhere," Lloyd said. "Not on any of the posters, or on the sign-up sheets."

"Maybe not, but everyone knows that's what we meant," Jessica said testily.

"All you said was that it started Thursday. Today's Thursday. In fact, it's been Thursday for seven hours, nine minutes, and forty-seven seconds already," Lloyd observed.

"No one else is starting now. Why do we have to?" Jessica argued.

"Maybe you should think about that the next time you advertise something," Lloyd said.

Jessica frowned. Wasn't there any way to get out of this?

"So I'll meet you by the front steps of school," Lloyd said. "And by the way, I like maple frosted doughnuts the best."

"Arrrrgh!" Jessica slammed the telephone back into the receiver on the wall.

"What's your problem?" asked Steven, Jessica's fourteen-year-old brother, coming down the stairs into the kitchen.

"*The Attack of the Geeks, Part Two*," Jessica grumbled. She turned to Elizabeth. "Do you believe Lloyd? Asking me to buy doughnuts for him?"

Elizabeth was moothing out and rolling up two neckties on the table. "That does seem kind of unreasonable."

"What are those ties for?" Steven asked. "Is it some kind of new middle-school fad? Girls wearing ugly ties?"

"No way would I wear one of these," Elizabeth said, laughing. "They're for two very special, very obnoxious guys."

"Can I have one?" Jessica asked.

"What for?" Elizabeth replied.

"I'm going to use it to strangle Lloyd!" Jessica said.

Mandy refastened her favorite barrette in her hair. It had little silk daisies across the top. She retied her pale-pink sweater around her waist. She wanted to make sure she looked her best, just in case she saw Peter before school.

She was sitting outside on the steps, waiting for Jim and Jessica to show up. Around her, kids were talking loudly. Occasionally there was a squeal, or a laugh, which she figured probably meant some of the masters were asking their servants to do particularly horrible things.

"Hi, Mandy. I'm reporting for duty." Jim stopped in front of her and smiled.

"Hi, Jim," Mandy said. "You know what? I haven't even thought of anything for you to do yet."

"Sounds good to me," Jim said. "Does this mean you're giving me the day off?"

"Well, not completely," Mandy said. "But you can have the morning off, anyway. Check with me at lunch. I might want to ask you to stand in the lunch line for me." She smiled. "Or take my math quiz this afternoon."

Jim laughed. "Trust me, you don't want me to do that. Not unless you're willing to risk getting a D. Math is not my best subject."

"OK, OK. I'll see you at lunch then," Mandy said.

"See you later." Jim went off to join his friends.

Mandy picked up a pebble and threw it down the steps. *Why is it so easy to talk to Jim, and so hard to talk to Peter?*

She smiled when she spotted Jessica on the lawn, walking over to Lloyd and handing him a bag with the name Daylight Doughnuts on it. They argued for a minute, and then Jessica walked over to where Mandy was sitting.

"What was that all about?" Mandy asked.

"Lloyd made me bring his breakfast," Jessica said, sitting beside Mandy. "Not only is he a nerd, he's a jerk. But don't worry. I'm not going to order *you* around all day."

"You're not?" Mandy asked. "You can if you want to. I mean, this is your big chance." She thought that Jessica would have a million things for her to do.

"I was thinking about it all last night," Jessica said. "And I decided there's only one thing I'm going to ask you to do."

"Only one?" Mandy said, her eyebrows shooting up in surprise. "What is it? Wait—let me guess." Mandy tapped her foot on the step. "Let's see . . . You want me to lend you this jacket, right? It's yours." She handed Jessica her purple-embroidered jean jacket. Jessica was always saying how much she wanted one just like it.

"No, it's not that." Jessica handed back the jacket. "It's something much more important than that." She smiled.

"More important than clothes? Hmmm, this is going to be tough," Mandy teased. "I know!" She snapped her fingers. "You want me to sneak into the principal's office and change the grades in your school record."

Jessica frowned. "My grades aren't *that* bad."

"I know, I was just kidding," Mandy said. "So what is it? I'm dying of suspense."

"OK. But before I tell you, you have to promise to do it, no matter what it is," Jessica said.

"Of course I will," Mandy said. Jessica sounded so serious, she was beginning to get a little worried. "That's part of the deal, right? I'm yours for the whole day—tomorrow, too. Go ahead—ask me anything!"

"Remember. No matter how hard it is, you only have to do *one* thing as my servant." Jessica took a deep breath and looked Mandy in the eye. "Before lunch today you have to ask Peter Jeffries to the Valentine's dance."

Mandy's jaw dropped in shock. "What?" she cried.

"You have to ask Peter to the dance."

"No! That's impossible! I *can't*." Mandy's heart was hammering in her chest just thinking about it. Ask Peter to the dance—before lunch? No way! "Jessica, that's not fair—I—"

"You promised," Jessica reminded her. "It's the only thing you have to do—after that you're a free woman."

"Please don't ask me to do that," Mandy begged. "Please?"

"Too late," Jessica said. "I already did."

* * *

"We want our servants to be well dressed," Amy said. "You guys do know how to knot your ties, don't you?"

Ken pulled the tie around his neck and examined the loud pink, orange, lime-green, and black geometric pattern. "This thing should be burned, not worn. It's almost as wide as my shirt!"

"Oh, come on—don't you love that psychedelic look?" Elizabeth asked.

"More like a psychotic look," Todd complained, examining the even uglier tie Elizabeth had given him as he looped it around and into a knot at his neck. The tie was one Elizabeth, Jessica, and Steven had given their father for Father's Day when they were little. It was bright yellow and orange, with tiny parrots on it. "I feel like an idiot," Todd said as he straightened out the ends of the tie.

Exactly the point, Elizabeth thought, smiling at him. "We'd better hurry, or we'll be late to English class."

"Couldn't you just ask us to carry you to class or something?" Ken complained to Amy on their way down the hall.

Todd was holding his books in front of his tie. "How about if we take you to Casey's for banana splits after school instead?"

"Come on. You guys look great," Amy said, holding the classroom door open for the boys.

As soon as Ken and Todd walked into the room, there was a burst of laughter.

"What happened to you guys?" Ellen asked, giggling.

"Presenting the top two candidates for the worst-dressed award in the yearbook!" Aaron yelled.

The bell rang, and Mr. Bowman loudly cleared his throat. "All right, let's get started. Ken and Todd, I'd like to ask you to come up to the board."

"What for?" Ken asked.

"Well, if you're going to wear such fashionable ties, you should be out here where everyone can see them." Mr. Bowman smiled. He was known for being both one of the nicest and also the worst-dressed teachers at school. He had a habit of wearing fish-pattern ties, and green-and-orange suit jackets.

"This is great," Elizabeth said to Amy as Ken and Todd shuffled up to the front of the room, hanging their heads.

"And this is only the beginning!" Amy said, smiling.

As Todd approached his desk, Mr. Bowman shook his head. "That tie is fantastic. I might just have to borrow it sometime."

"How about now?" Todd started to take it off.

"No way!" Elizabeth called out. "You're not allowed to. You're my servant, remember? I get to tell you what to wear."

Todd groaned. "Do I have to wear this tomorrow, too?"

"No, my dad has an even uglier one I'm bringing in for you tomorrow," Elizabeth said. "I think it's made of Velcro."

Everyone started laughing again.

"This master-servant thing is turning out to be a blast," Elizabeth heard Danny Jackson say.

"Speak for yourself," Ken replied, flipping the tie over his shoulder.

Five

◇

Mandy peered into the mirror above the bathroom sink and quickly rubbed off a tiny ink mark on her cheek. She was glad she had decided to check her appearance before she talked to Peter. It was going to be embarrassing enough without ink on her face.

She took a small dark-blue eyeliner pencil out of her purse and drew a very thin line just under her bottom lashes. She didn't usually wear makeup to school, but today was special. Then she took a few steps backward and checked to make sure her shirt was tucked in right.

She smiled at the mirror. "Hi, Peter," she practiced, trying to sound cool and calm.

"Did you just say something?" Julie Porter asked, stepping out of one of the stalls.

Mandy blushed. "No. I mean, I was just talking to myself."

Julie laughed. "I talk to mirrors all the time," she teased. "Mirror, mirror, on the wall . . . don't make me go to study hall."

Mandy smiled and stuffed her brush into her purse. "Wish me luck, OK?"

"Why? What's up?" Julie asked.

"I'm about to make a fool out of myself," Mandy said.

Julie studied her for a moment. "Well, you'll look good making a fool of yourself, anyway," she said.

"Thanks." Mandy walked out of the bathroom.

Maybe this is a good thing, she thought as she walked down the hall. *Maybe I should thank Jessica. Maybe Peter will say yes. Maybe we'll go to the dance and have an incredible time together. Maybe . . .* She had to stop thinking about it. It was making her so nervous, she could feel her heart pounding in her chest.

She had only one more period before lunch, and she had to ask him before then. She decided to drop by Peter's locker casually to see if he was there.

She spotted him hanging out by Bruce's locker, talking to him and a group of their friends. *He's busy,* she thought. *Besides, I can't ask him in front of all those other people.*

But at that moment Peter turned away and walked down to his own locker. *It's now or never,*

Mandy told herself, trying to think confidently. *Just do it.*

She walked up to Peter and almost went right past him, she was so nervous. Then she stopped and turned around. "Oh, hi," she said, trying to sound casual, as if she'd just bumped into him. So what if Peter's locker was actually at the end of the hall, not on the way to anywhere? She didn't need to worry about that right now.

"Hi, Mandy. What's up?" Peter tossed one book into his locker and took out another.

"Oh, nothing much." She shrugged. "How do you like the servant thing? Is Lila making you work hard?"

"Not really," Peter said. "I think she has so many servants at home, there isn't much left for me to do. Though she did say something about my running some errands for her later."

"Uh-oh," Mandy said. "Watch out. She'll probably make you carry her home on your shoulders or something."

Peter laughed.

This is going so well, Mandy thought. *I can't believe I'm actually talking to Peter and not tripping over every word.*

Now came the hard part—the bell was going to ring any second. "So, Peter, not to change the subject or anything, but I was wondering," Mandy began, staring at the floor. She was so nervous, she felt as if she were going to faint. "Would you . . . uh . . . like to go with me on Saturday?"

Peter looked confused. "Go where?"

"Oh." Mandy blushed. "Right. Uh . . . I meant, to the Valentine's dance. Whether you would go with me to that." *Really smooth, Mandy*, she thought miserably.

Mandy was so nervous about Peter's answer, it seemed as if it took him about an hour to say anything. He finally smiled and caught her eye. "Thanks for asking me," he said. "I mean, that's really nice."

Mandy felt her heart leap. *He said yes! I can't belive it!*

Peter cleared his throat. "But I already have a date." He shrugged just as the bell rang. "I'm really sorry."

Mandy felt her heart plunge right down to her high-top sneakers. "Oh. That's OK," she said quietly.

She turned around and practically ran down the hallway. She had to get out of there as fast as she could. She couldn't let Peter see how upset and embarrassed she was.

No big deal, she kept telling herself as she walked to her locker. *It's not that big a deal*. But she knew it was. She'd never be able to look Peter in the face again.

I never should have asked him, she told herself as she threw open her locker. *I knew I shouldn't have asked him. Why did I ever think it was OK to ask him?*

Her mouth hardened into an angry line as she took out her English books and slammed her locker shut. She asked Peter to the dance because Jessica Wakefield made her ask Peter to the dance. Now she'd made a complete and total fool of herself, and it was all Jessica's fault.

Jessica stood in the lunch line on Thursday and tapped her fingernails against the red plastic tray. "First it was his breakfast, now it's his lunch," she muttered.

"Did you say something?" asked Charlie Cashman, who was standing in front of her.

"No," Jessica snapped. *Lloyd's driving me so crazy, I'm starting to talk to myself!* She was reaching for a dish of lime Jell-O when she felt a tap on her arm. "What do you want now, Lloyd?" she demanded, turning around.

"An apology," Mandy said. She looked so angry, Jessica took a step backward and bumped into the stack of lunch trays.

"What happened?" Jessica asked. "Or shouldn't I ask?"

"Total disaster, that's what happened," Mandy said. "You made me ask Peter, so I did. I hope you're happy." She turned from the line and stomped toward the Unicorner.

"He said . . . no?" Jessica asked hesitantly, leaving her place in line to follow Mandy.

"Worse than that. He said he already *has* a date," Mandy said without even looking back at her. "Don't you think you could have found that out before you made me humiliate myself in front of him?"

"I'm sorry!" Jessica said, grabbing her arm and pulling her to a stop. "I didn't know he had a date."

"Are you sure?" Mandy put her hands on her hips. "Because if that was your idea of a joke, it was pretty cruel!"

"It wasn't, I swear!" Jessica said. "I had no idea. I *never* would have asked you to ask him if I knew that."

"You didn't ask me, you *ordered* me," Mandy reminded Jessica.

"Mandy, you have to believe me. I didn't make you do it to be mean. I just wanted you guys to go to the dance together," Jessica told her. "I was trying to help! I thought this would be the perfect way to get you two together. Or to speed it up, at least."

"It sped things up, all right," Mandy grumbled, folding her arms across her chest. "It sped them up so fast, they went right off the end of a cliff."

"I'm really sorry, Mandy," Jessica said. "I know how much you like him. It was a stupid thing to make you do, OK? How about this? You can have the rest of the day off. I won't ask you anything else. You can have tomorrow off, too."

"Like that's going to help!" Mandy turned around again and stormed off.

Jessica stared after her. She'd never seen Mandy so angry and upset before. She had to think of some way she could make it up to her friend—and fast.

"No, on your hands," Elizabeth said. "Like this." She got down on her hands and knees and pressed into a handstand. Then she started walking down the hall, one hand in front of the other.

"Way to go, Elizabeth!" Amy applauded her.

Elizabeth dropped her feet down, stood up, and took a little bow. "Now you guys do the same thing—only you have to walk across the lunchroom like that."

"I'm not very good at gymnastics," Todd said. "Can't I do something else instead?"

"Couldn't we just serve you lunch?" Ken suggested. "We'll get whatever you want, we'll bring it to your table—"

"No." Amy shook her head.

Todd groaned. "How is *us* walking across the lunchroom on our hands going to help *you*?" he asked.

"Good question," Elizabeth said. "Let's just say

that it'll . . . provide us with amusement."

"Lots of amusement," Amy added.

"We're only supposed to be your servants, not your personal comedians," Ken grumbled. "No one else is doing stupid stunts like this."

Elizabeth shrugged. "What can we say? We're original. Now, hurry up and get in there before lunch is over with." She held open the door.

Slowly, Ken and Todd got onto the floor and lifted their legs into the air. It took Todd about five tries to stay upright on his hands.

"His legs are too long," Amy whispered to Elizabeth, giggling.

As the boys entered the lunchroom, a few kids laughed as they passed by their tables, but a lot of people were so busy eating, they didn't even seem to notice. Elizabeth decided something had to be done about that.

"Attention! Attention!" she called in a loud voice. "Presenting the incredible lunchroom acrobats—Ken Matthews and Todd Wilkins!"

Todd glared at her upside down, the ugly tie he was still wearing dragging across the linoleum floor. Then he seemed to get confused about which direction he was supposed to go. He turned in a circle, his high-top sneakers towering above his head, as his face turned a deeper and deeper shade of pink.

He had just started moving forward again and was getting close to the other end of the lunchroom when Mr. Clark, the principal, walked in the far doors. Todd, unable to see where he was going, kept on walking and crashed right into Mr. Clark.

Elizabeth and Amy burst out laughing just as Ken, startled by the noise, bumped into a chair and fell over. Everyone in the lunchroom stood up and started clapping.

"Todd, Ken, what in the world are you doing?" Mr. Clark asked, brushing off his trousers from where Todd's sneakers had smacked into his leg.

"Way to go, Wilkins!" a group of Todd's friends yelled at the same time.

"Let's see that again!"

"Anyone got a video camera?"

Todd and Ken quietly slunk out of the lunchroom.

Mr. Clark walked over to where Amy and Elizabeth were standing. "Elizabeth, do you have any idea what those two are up to?" he asked her, shaking his head in disbelief.

Elizabeth shrugged. "I really don't know what's gotten into them. Do you, Amy?"

"No idea," Amy said. "But they sure are acting strange, aren't they?"

"Why don't you just ask someone else?" Ellen suggested.

Mandy made a face. "I don't want to go with anybody else," she said. "Besides, it would be humiliating to see Peter there, now that he knows I wanted to go with him." She pushed around the taco salad on her plate. "I just won't go."

She'd been avoiding even looking in Peter's direction ever since he came into the lunchroom. It was bad enough that he turned her down, but to know he'd already asked someone else to the dance was even worse. It meant he liked someone else, and that she didn't have a chance with him. And now he had to go and sit two tables away from her!

"Don't let it get to you," Mary advised. "You know there are tons of other guys who'd like to take you to the dance."

"Yeah, tons of cute guys," Belinda said.

"Oh, come on. It's Thursday," Mandy said. "Even if I did want one, I'm not going to get a date before Saturday."

"Why not? I don't have one, but I'm not worried about it," Belinda said. "I figure Jim and I will get around to asking each other sooner or later. Speaking of which, what have you made him do today?"

"Nothing," Mandy grumbled. "I'm sick of this whole stupid master-servant game."

"Mandy! It was your idea, and we're raising a lot of money," Mary reminded her.

"Yeah, and it could be a lot worse," Lila said.

"Be glad you're not Janet. Right now she's rehears-ing *Romeo and Juliet* with Winston, and he's making her play Juliet."

Belinda shrugged. "It's better than Romeo."

"Jessica has it pretty rough, too," Mary said. "I heard Lloyd made her eat the meat loaf surprise for lunch, so he could measure how sick it made a human feel."

Mandy dropped her fork on her plate and pushed her tray away. "As far as I'm concerned, Jessica got what she deserved," she said.

Mandy knew Jessica wasn't normally a mean person, but she couldn't help feeling that her friend had set her up. Jessica had made her do the thing she least wanted to do in the whole world—and her worst fears about doing it had come true.

She heard some people laughing, and she turned to see what was going on in the middle of the lunchroom. Peter was looking her way, and their eyes met for a brief second. Mandy hurriedly looked away. She felt her face turn red.

It was all because of Jessica that she was feeling so miserable. She looked over to where Jessica was forcing down her last big bite of meat loaf surprise. *I hope Lloyd makes her eat the mushy green beans, too.*

"Hey, Elizabeth, can I ask you something?"

Aaron Dallas caught up with her outside school later that afternoon.

"Sure."

"Do you know much about the rules of this master-servant thing?" Aaron asked.

"A little bit," Elizabeth answered. "Why? What's up?"

Aaron slung his backpack over his shoulder. "Well, I was wondering if maybe I could switch with someone, so that I could end up having Jessica as my servant," Aaron said. He looked slightly embarrassed. "Don't get me wrong. I like Grace Oliver and everything. It's just that I know how miserable Jessica is, having to answer to Lloyd."

"What's he been doing?" Elizabeth asked.

"He made her eat all this gross food for lunch today," Aaron said. "And this afternoon she has to help him with some chemistry experiments. He told her that tomorrow he's planning even more stuff."

"Poor Jessica," Elizabeth said. She had it almost as bad as Ken and Todd did, working for her and Amy.

"So, anyway, I was thinking, maybe I could switch with Lloyd somehow and give Jessica a break," Aaron said. "I thought it could be my Valentine's present to her."

Elizabeth sighed. *At least someone around here is feeling romantic,* she thought wistfully. "That's really nice," she said.

"So what do you think? Can I just ask him, or do I have to arrange it with Mandy or something?" Aaron asked. "I kind of want to keep it a secret."

"I'm not sure. I think Lloyd's out for revenge after that whole earthquake disaster," Elizabeth said. "I doubt you'll be able to talk *him* out of bossing Jessica around."

"Oh, well." Aaron sighed. "Maybe you're right. Lloyd probably isn't going to want to switch. I wanted to help, but I guess she's stuck with him."

"Sorry," Elizabeth said.

"That's OK," Aaron said. "I'll just have to think of another present, if this doesn't work out. Thanks for the advice." He waved. "I'll see you tomorrow."

Elizabeth watched Aaron get onto his bike. *Why can't Todd be as sweet as that?* she wondered. *Why does he have to act like a two-year-old?*

Six

◇

"You know, Peter is my servant, after all. If I wanted to, I could order him to take you to the Valentine's dance," Lila said to Mandy.

It was Thursday afternoon, and she and Mandy were walking over to Lila's house for a swim in the Fowlers' huge deluxe pool.

Mandy's eyes grew big and round. "No way!" she protested. "Whatever you do, don't do that."

"Why not?" Lila asked. "I mean, what good is having power if you can't use it to get what you want?"

"No wonder you Fowlers are so successful in business," Mandy said, shaking her head. "In the first place, the dance is Saturday, and your *power* over Peter runs out on Friday. And in the second place, that would be completely, utterly embarrassing. So don't even *think* about it."

"OK, OK!" Lila cried. "I was just trying to help." She flipped her long, shiny hair over her shoulder. "Personally, I think you should pay Jessica back for being so mean to you today," Lila said.

"Believe me, I'd like to," Mandy said. "There's nothing worse than getting dumped by someone before you even go out with him. He probably thinks I'm a total loser now. And the whole thing is Jessica's fault, even if she didn't mean to do it."

"That's just it," Lila said. "Whether she meant it or not, you *were* humiliated."

"Thanks for pointing that out," Mandy said wryly.

"And you have to do something about it," Lila said. "I think she deserves a little, you know, payback, or whatever you call it."

"Revenge?"

"Right." Lila shifted her leather backpack from one shoulder to the other.

Mandy knew that Lila and Jessica were usually competing or feuding with each other in some way, even though they were best friends. She could tell that Lila was going to have a lot of fun helping her get back at Jessica. But even if Lila did have her own reasons for getting Jessica, Mandy knew she was right. Jessica did deserve some kind of retaliation for making her ask Peter to the dance—something big. "So what did you have in mind?" Mandy asked Lila as they turned into the long driveway up to the Fowler mansion.

"Well, you know how Elizabeth and Amy are making Ken and Todd do all that idiotic stuff to get back at them for that practical joke?" Lila asked.

Mandy nodded. "Yeah. They looked pretty ridiculous today." She laughed, remembering Todd's face when he bumped into Mr. Clark in the lunchroom. It had been the only thing that had made her laugh all day.

"So . . . all you have to do is switch with Lloyd, and *you* could be Jessica's boss," Lila said, pulling open the enormous front door of the house. "Then you can make her do anything you want."

"No." Mandy shook her head. "I can't ask Lloyd to switch with me."

"Why not? He'll do anything you ask," Lila said, stepping into the hallway. "He's a nerd—you're a Unicorn. He'll probably be thrilled you're even talking to him."

"Nope. Lloyd's the last person who'd do me a favor," Mandy said. "Don't you remember that time I was imitating him intthe lunchroom a few months ago, and he walked in? He practically died on the spot." Lloyd had looked as if he wanted to kill her when he'd caught Mandy wearing someone else's glasses, with her pants hiked up and about fifteen pencils in her blouse pocket.

"Oh, right," Lila said. "That was hilarious, but I guess you're right. Lloyd's not exactly going to be on your side."

"Besides that, he's having such a good time torturing Jessica," Mandy pointed out as she followed Lila into the kitchen. "Not that I blame him. . . ."

"OK, so asking Lloyd is definitely out." Lila put her backpack on the floor and opened the refrigerator. She took out two cans of soda and handed one to Mandy. "Maybe there's another way we can get Jessica to be your servant."

Mandy took a sip of soda. "I can't think of anything."

"Well, we will," Lila said. "Trust me."

"Where have you been all afternoon?" Mrs. Wakefield asked Jessica when she walked in the front door just before dinner Thursday night. The rest of the family was already sitting at the dinner table.

"Doing chemistry experiments," Jessica said, pulling out her chair. "Can you believe it?"

Her father grinned. "Actually, no."

"A very important experiment," Steven said. "She was mixing different kinds of nail polish together. She found out that blue and red make purple," he joked. He helped himself to a huge spoonful of mashed potatoes.

Jessica glared at him. "Don't even think about

giving me a hard time. I've had a completely rotten day. Even you can't make it much worse."

"Lloyd made you do chemistry experiments all afternoon?" Elizabeth asked.

Jessica shook her head. "*He* did the experiments. *I* had to write down all the stupid results. He thinks he's going to win the Nobel prize or something."

"This is all because of the master-servant day the Unicorns organized to raise money for the hospital?" Mrs. Wakefield asked.

Jessica nodded. Her parents had agreed to add a hundred dollars to the Unicorns' donation to the hospital. "Not just one day," she grumbled. "It's tomorrow, too."

"I know," Elizabeth said, smiling. "I can't wait."

"Sure, *you're* having fun." Jessica stabbed a tomato with her fork. Elizabeth was having a blast making Ken and Todd do stupid things. And it was all thanks to her. If she hadn't cheated for Elizabeth . . . "Wait a second," she said out loud, the tomato halfway to her mouth.

"What is it?" her father asked. "Something wrong with the salad?"

"No." Jessica felt her appetite start to perk up. After that meat loaf for lunch, she'd thought she would never eat again. "Elizabeth, remember that favor I did for you yesterday?"

"Yeah. Um . . ." Elizabeth was looking a little uneasy. "Thanks again."

"You're welcome again," Jessica said, tearing off a piece of bread. She could tell her sister was nervous that her parents might find out she had cheated, so she made sure she didn't give anything away. "But remember how I said you'd owe me a favor now?"

Elizabeth nodded. She was starting to look a little suspicious. "What is it?"

"I need you to switch with me. I need you to be Lloyd's servant tomorrow, instead of me," Jessica said. "Who are you supposed to be working for again?"

"Belinda," Elizabeth said. "But, Jessica—"

"A favor deserves a favor, right?" Jessica asked. "One good turn deserves another and all that."

"Yeah, but my favor didn't hurt you," Elizabeth said. "I don't want to help Lloyd with his chemistry set tomorrow!"

"Join the club," Jessica said. "Neither do I. But now, thanks to you, I won't have to!"

"I'm free!" Jessica announced to Lila on the telephone later that night. "Isn't that fantastic? No more Lloyd, no more doughnut delivery, no more—"

"That's great," Lila interrupted. "But listen to this." She cleared her throat. "I was talking to Peter earlier."

"Peter Jeffries?" Jessica asked. She felt bad just hearing his name.

"Yeah. I called him, pretending to ask him to do some stuff as my servant," Lila explained. "Then I just casually brought up the topic of the dance."

"You're kidding," Jessica said. "What did he say? Did he tell you who he's going with?"

"Excuse me, can I get a word in?" Lila asked.

"Oh. Sorry," Jessica said.

"He's going to the dance with Grace Oliver," Lila said.

"Grace!" Jessica exclaimed. "He's going with Grace?"

"Why not? What's wrong with Grace?" Lila asked, sounding confused.

"Oh . . . nothing," Jessica said. "I'm just surprised, that's all. You'd think she would have told us already. I mean, wouldn't you be thrilled if Peter asked you to the dance?"

"Maybe he didn't ask her. Maybe she asked him," Lila suggested.

"So what? He's still a great date."

"Do *you* want to go out with him? Does that have something to do with why you made Mandy embarrass herself today?"

"No way! I'm not interested in him," Jessica said hotly. "I'm just saying he's very cute and all that." Jessica shook her head. "Wow. Grace Oliver. I could have found that out before I told Mandy to ask Peter to the dance." Grace was in the Unicorn Club, too, and Jessica was pretty good friends with her. She was surprised she hadn't heard about Grace and Peter, but then again, Grace had been home sick a few days last week when they were planning their fund-raiser. In fact, Grace probably didn't even know Mandy liked Peter.

"That's right," Lila said in a snotty voice. "You sure could have. Then you would have spared Mandy a lot of pain and embarrassment."

"I know." Jessica twisted the phone cord around her finger. "I feel so terrible about what happened. I really want to make it up to Mandy."

"She's still pretty mad at you, you know," Lila said. "And I can't say I blame her. That was a pretty rotten trick."

"It wasn't a trick! I didn't mean for it to work out the way it did," Jessica said. "Anyway, can you think of anything I could do to cheer her up?"

Lila sighed dramatically. "I don't know, Jessica. I don't think she's going to forgive you anytime soon."

"Well, thanks for all the help, Lila," Jessica said sourly. "Listen, I have to go . . . clear the table. I'll see you tomorrow."

After she'd hung up the phone, Jessica went and lay facedown on her bed. She hated the thought of

Mandy being so mad at her. All she'd been trying to do was help. Everything had gone wrong.

The only way to make it up to Mandy would be if she could get Mandy and Peter together somehow. But they couldn't go to the Valentine's dance—that would mean Peter would have to dump Grace, and Grace's feelings would be hurt. She didn't want that to happen.

What else can I do? If she didn't think of something soon, she had a feeling *all* of the Unicorns were going to be mad at her.

Mandy pressed the channel button on the remote control. If she saw one more music video of a love song, she was going to throw up. For the past hour she'd been trying to watch television, but for some reason everything ended up reminding her of Peter. Normally Mandy didn't like to mope around the house, but today was an exception. She kept remembering the look on Peter's face when he told her he already had a date for the dance—and how stupid she must have seemed.

That was the last time she was going to ask anyone to anything. Ever!

"Mandy! Telephone!" her mother called from upstairs.

Mandy turned off the TV and ran into the kitchen to pick up the phone.

It was Lila.

"Listen, I just talked to Jessica, and I have great news," Lila said.

"I don't know if I want to hear any great news about Jessica," Mandy responded.

"No—it's good news for you, not for her. You're not going to believe this. Jessica switched masters with Elizabeth, so now Lloyd is Elizabeth's boss, and Belinda is her boss," Lila told Mandy.

"Uh-huh." Mandy stared at the ceiling. Her mind was already wandering back to Peter.

"You know what that means, don't you?" Lila asked eagerly.

"No," Mandy said.

"Now instead of trying to get Lloyd to switch with you, you could trade with Belinda. She and Jim like each other, so he'd probably be happy to work for her. Then Jessica would be *your* servant!" Lila said triumphantly.

Mandy grinned. "Wow, Lila. You're brilliant."

"I know," Lila said. "Now, let's talk about what you can do to Jessica."

Seven

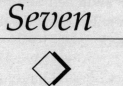

"Hi, Belinda. I'm reporting for duty," Jessica said cheerfully when she saw Belinda outside on the school steps Friday morning. "Elizabeth told you we switched, right?"

Belinda nodded. "She called me last night. But—"

Jessica skipped around in a small circle. "I'm in such a good mood, I'll do anything you ask—I'll even walk across the lunchroom on my hands to get your lunch."

Belinda laughed. "You don't need to do that. Anyway—"

"Are you sure?" Jessica asked. "Anything you want, free of charge. Service with a smile. Just ask."

"Well, I'd love to ask you to do lots of stuff for me, but I can't," Belinda said.

"Come on." Jessica playfully punched Belinda's

shoulder. "Don't be shy. It's no problem. Really."

"No, it's not that," Belinda said, laughing. "I can't ask you to do anything because you're not my servant anymore."

"But we only switched last night," Jessica said. "Did you switch with someone else after that?"

Belinda nodded.

"Who?"

"Mandy."

Jessica's eyebrows shot up. "M-Mandy?" she sputtered. She'd gotten rid of Lloyd and gotten Mandy as a replacement? She knew there was only one reason Mandy had made the switch, and that was to get back at her for the day before. Having Mandy as a master was even *worse* than having Lloyd. *But it's partly my fault,* Jessica reminded herself. *If I hadn't been such a bad boss to her, she wouldn't be getting me back now.*

"Don't worry, I'm sure it won't be too terrible," Belinda said just as Jim walked over to her.

Jessica hoisted her backpack onto her shoulder. "Don't be so sure," she said. "Anyway, I'll see you guys later."

On her way across the school lawn, she practically bumped right into Lila, who had just been dropped off by her father's chauffeur.

"Did you hear the good news?" Lila asked. "You're Mandy's servant now."

Jessica smiled faintly. "Yeah, I know."

"I helped her arrange it," Lila said with a smirk. "Because I knew how much you wanted to get away from Lloyd."

Jessica gave her a suspicious look. Why did she get the feeling that Lila was behind this whole thing? Lila was the only one she'd told about her switch with Elizabeth the night before. It didn't have an l thing to do with helping *Jessica* out, that was for sure. If Lila was helping Mandy, then she really was in big trouble. "Gee, thanks," she said, giving Lila a phony smile. "You're such a good friend."

"Anything to help," Lila said, miling back at her.

Jessica sighed and turned to go into school. She was halfway up the steps when Aaron came out the front door. She tried to smile at him.

Aaron stopped on the step above her. "Did you hear the good news yet?" he asked.

"Good news?" Jessica asked. "Which good news?" So far the good news she'd been hearing was anything but good.

"Didn't Lloyd tell you? I switched servants with him last night," Aaron said, stepping down so he was level with her. "I knew how unhappy you were getting ordered around by him. I didn't think Lloyd was going to agree to switch, but then he started muttering all this stuff about Saint Valentine, and how mystical and historical it all was. You know

Lloyd." He smiled shyly. "Anyway, you know what that means."

"Uh . . . not really," Jessica said.

"Jessica! It means you're free. You're not Lloyd's servant anymore, you're mine." Aaron smiled. "Don't worry, I won't be half as bad as Lloyd."

Jessica just shook her head in disbelief. This was terrible! If she had just stuck with Lloyd, everything would be great. Instead, she had made things ten times worse! And it was so incredibly sweet of Aaron to come to her rescue like that. It was so romantic, his switching with Lloyd. But it didn't even matter!

"Jessica?" Aaron said. "You don't look too happy about this."

Jessica groaned. "It's not that. It was so nice of you to switch. But I already switched with Elizabeth last night," she explained.

Aaron's smile faded. "You did?"

Jessica nodded. "I did. Now she's your servant, and I'm Mandy's because she switched with Belinda."

"So . . . can't you switch back?" Aaron asked, sounding confused.

Jessica shook her head. "Mandy will never let me. She's really mad at me. She switched on purpose to get me back for ordering her to ask Peter Jeffries to the dance."

"Oh." Aaron looked disappointed and totally perplexed.

"But thanks for trying to help me," Jessica said, smiling at him. "I wish it had worked out." She started back up the steps, then turned around. "We're still going to the dance together, right?"

"Sure," Aaron said with a shrug. He looked so sad, Jessica wanted to cry. If she hadn't forced Elizabeth to switch with her, right now she'd be Aaron's servant instead of Mandy's, and her life would be a hundred percent better.

Whose idea was this stupid master-servant thing, anyway? she thought angrily. The longer it lasted, the more of a nightmare it became!

"With all the switches going on around here, you'd think Ken and Todd would have tried to switch, too," Amy said to Elizabeth before science class Friday morning.

"I know," Elizabeth said. "I wonder why they didn't. Did Ken call you last night to complain or anything?"

"No," Amy said.

"Neither did Todd," Elizabeth said. "Oh, well. Maybe they're not really as upset as they seemed yesterday."

"Yeah, maybe. But are you sure we're not going too far, making them do more stupid stunts today?

I mean, maybe we've gotten them back enough already," Amy said.

"What makes you say that?" Elizabeth asked. "Aren't you enjoying this?"

"Sure," Amy said. "It's just . . . well, I really do want to go to the dance with Ken. I don't want him to get so mad at me that he never wants to see me again."

"For someone who usually makes fun of Jessica for being all goofy about boys, you sure are acting a little . . . lovesick," Elizabeth teased.

"I am not!" Amy cried. "I just want to go to the dance, that's all. Everyone's going to be there."

"True," Elizabeth said. "Uh-oh. Look. Here they come," she warned Amy as she saw Ken and Todd coming down the hall. "Hi, guys." She waved nervously. Maybe Amy's lovesickness was catching, she thought. She couldn't help noticing how cute Todd looked today.

"OK, I can tell you guys are plotting against us agiin," Todd said. He grinned. "Go ahead. Give us our next order."

Elizabeth couldn't believe what a good sport Todd was being, especially after Mr. Clark had lectured him yesterday afternoon about not horsing around in school. *What's gotten into him?* she wondered.

"Yeah, what's the next assignment?" Ken asked Amy, smiling at her.

Amy looked at Elizabeth. The expression on her face seemed to be saying, *Should we still make them do this? They're being so nice!*

But Elizabeth wasn't going to let them off so easy. *She* wasn't going to be taken in by all that romantic Valentine's Day stuff. She wasn't going to forget the bucket of ice water down her back. "OK, here's the deal. You guys have to raise your hands to answer every question Ms. Blake asks—and you have to answer it wrong, whether you know the right answer or not."

"You're kidding," Ken said.

Elizabeth shook her head.

"You're not kidding," Todd said. He shrugged. "Well, OK. That doesn't sound too bad."

"Not too bad? But Ms. Blake hates it when people don't know the answer," Ken said. "She makes those little black marks in her attendance book."

Elizabeth saw Todd nudge Ken in the ribs, and they exchanged a look. *What was that all about?* she wondered.

"But hey. Who cares about Ms. Blake? Anyway, it's only one class," Ken said with a shrug.

The bell rang, and they filed into the classroom and took their seats.

"Good morning, class." Ms. Blake smiled. "Today we'll be continuing our discussion of plant life. Now, can anyone tell me the scientific term for the process that plants use to turn light into energy?"

Ken raised his hand immediately.

"Yes, Ken?" Ms. Blake seemed surprised that Ken was so eager to answer. He didn't usually like to participate in class.

"Mouth-to-mouth resuscitation?" Ken answered.

Everyone in the classroom started laughing. Elizabeth had to cover her mouth, she was giggling so hard.

Ms. Blake raised one eyebrow. "No . . . " she said slowly. "Not even close. Would anyone else like to give it a try?"

Todd raised his hand.

"All right, Todd. Surely you can do better than that," Ms. Blake said, making a mark in her grade book with a black pen.

"Photo . . . photo . . ." Todd hesitated.

Ms. Blake waved her arms in the air, encouraging Todd to continue the word.

"Photo finish?"

Ms. Blake shook her head and picked up the pen again.

"Can I carry your books? Do you want me to clean out your locker? How about if I make some valentines for you to hand out?" Jessica asked Mandy eagerly. "Pink, white, red? Ask me anything."

Mandy turned from her locker and gave Jessica

a stern look. "Don't talk to me about valentines," she said.

"Right. Sorry," Jessica apologized. "Really, incredibly sorry."

Mandy tried to hide a smile. She was actually having fun watching Jessica squirm.

"Isn't there anything you want me to do?" Jessica asked. "I mean, you did switch to be my boss and all. And I do want to make it up to you— you know, for what happened yesterday. I've been trying to think of something I could do. Just tell me. Should I ask Peter to break his date with Grace? I will, you know."

Mandy shook her head. "No. I wouldn't do that to Grace. Anyway, you've kind of done enough in that department."

Jessica scuffed the floor with her shoe. "Well . . . then what can I do? Practically the whole morning's gone by already."

"I know," Mandy said. "I've been trying to think of what I should have you do. I'm pretty sure I'm going to repay the favor you did me."

"Huh?" Jessica asked. "You want me to ask Peter to the dance? But I'm already going with Aaron."

"No, not that," Mandy said, tossing a notebook into her locker and shutting the door. She turned to face Jessica. "Just like you, I'm only going to ask *you* to do one thing."

"Sure," Jessica said, nodding. "So what is it?"

The bell rang, signaling the start of class. "I'll tell you at lunch," Mandy said. She started running down the hall.

"Tell me now!" Jessica called, running after her. "Come on, I'm dying to find out."

"You'll find out in an hour," Mandy said, just before she ducked into her classroom.

"Sorry the servant switch didn't work out the way you wanted it to," Elizabeth told Aaron, catching up to him in the lunch line. "I never thought Lloyd would switch with you."

"That's OK." Aaron shrugged. "So I guess you're my servant now, huh? But first, before I forget—" He handed Elizabeth two envelopes.

Elizabeth looked at them suspiciously. "What are these?"

"Invitations to tomorrow's dance from Ken and Todd," Aaron said. He put a slice of pizza on his tray.

Elizabeth turned over the envelopes and examined both sides. "This isn't going to explode on me or anything, is it? Ken and Todd didn't ask you to make me do anything terrible?" Elizabeth asked.

Aaron shook his head. "Nope. Not at all. They just wanted me to give you those invitations." He picked up a heart-shaped cupcake and added it to his tray.

"Hmmm." *Maybe Aaron is starting to rub off on them. Maybe they decided to give up the practical jokes once and for all.* "Well, thanks, I guess," Elizabeth said. "Is there anything you want *me* to do?"

"Could you give this to Jessica?" Aaron pulled a large red envelope out of the math book under his arm. "I didn't put my name on it. It's supposed to be anonymous, so I thought maybe you could stick it in her locker."

"Sure," Elizabeth said. "I'd be glad to. Anything else?"

Aaron shook his head. "Nope. That's it. Thanks."

Elizabeth walked over to where Amy was sitting and handed her the envelope with her name on it. "Check it out—formal invitations."

"From who?" Amy asked.

"Who else?" Elizabeth replied, opening hers. Inside was a red card with white lace around the edges. Elizabeth skimmed the loopy, dramatic writing on it quickly. "Kind of overboard for Ken and Todd, isn't it?"

"What do you mean?" Amy was smiling as she read the card.

"Come on, they're never like this," Elizabeth said. "Their idea of an invitation is more like, 'So will you go with me or what?' This is a whole poem."

Amy sighed. "I know. Isn't it beautiful?"

"Amy! What's gotten into you? Do you actually

think Ken and Todd mean this?" Elizabeth asked.

"Of course," Amy said dreamily. "They're just trying to get into the Valentine spirit."

"The Valentine spirit?"

"Whatever." Amy studied the card again, a wistful smile on her face. "Sometimes Ken is so great, isn't he?"

"Yeah, *some*times," Elizabeth said.

Maybe I'm being too suspicious, Elizabeth told herself. *Maybe they really are being sincere.* She glanced over to where Ken and Todd were sitting, each of them wearing hideous wide ties.

But why would they be so nice after the way we've been treating them lately?

Eight

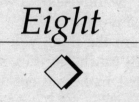

"Where is she?" Lila asked, looking around the lunchroom. "She must be stalling."

Mandy laughed. "If I were her, I would be, too. And she doesn't even know what we have planned yet."

"Poor Jessica," Mary said. "This is going to be torture."

"I know," Mandy said. "But you know what? I think it's going to be fun—for us, anyway."

"Is Aaron here?" Lila asked.

"Right over there." Ellen pointed to a table. "Jessica's not with him."

"Here she comes," Mary said, gesturing to the door.

Jessica rushed up to the table. "Sorry I'm late," she said breathlessly. "I had to stay after in English class and talk to Mr. Bowman about a book report I'm doing next week." She stared at Mandy's tray. "Oh, no—you already got your lunch. I was going to do that."

"That's OK," Mandy said. "I wasn't going to ask you to do that, anyway."

"But I thought the thing you wanted me to do had to do with lunch," Jessica said. She made a face. "You won't make me eat leftover meat loaf surprise, will you?"

"No, nothing like that," Mandy assured her. "Your assignment has to do with lunch, but it doesn't involve eating in any way."

"Except maybe eating crow," Lila muttered under her breath.

"What did you say?" Jessica asked.

"Nothing," Lila said.

Mandy stifled a laugh. "OK. I told you I only want you to do one thing, right?"

Jessica nodded.

"Well, I want you to sing. Now. In front of everybody."

"Everybody at the table?" Jessica asked.

"Everybody in this room," Mandy said. "You have to go out into the middle of the floor, get down on one knee, and sing as loud as you can, for at least three minutes."

Jessica looked as if she wanted to die, or at least

disappear. *Now she knows how I felt yesterday,* Mandy thought.

"What do I have to sing?" Jessica asked.

"I haven't decided that yet," Mandy said. "Do you guys have any suggestions?" She turned to the other Unicorns.

"How about the national anthem?" Ellen suggested.

Mandy shook her head. "Too boring."

" 'Happy Birthday'?" Mary proposed.

"Too easy," Lila said. "It should be something romantic, for Valentine's Day." She drummed her fingernails on the table. "I know! How about that cheesy old song Mrs. Pervis always sings, 'Feelings'?"

"How does it go?" Jessica asked. Lila hummed a few bars of the song, and Jessica's right eyebrow shot up. "Not *that* song."

"Why not? It'll be perfect," Mandy said. "It'll get everyone in the mood for the dance tomorrow."

"But—that's elevator music," Jessica protested. "Besides, I don't know all the words."

"So make them up," Mandy said.

"Jessica, you'd better get out there now, while everyone's still here," Lila said.

Jessica gave Mandy one last pleading look. "Couldn't I just sing it to you guys?"

"You have such a great singing voice, I think *every-*one should hear it," Mandy replied, smiling at her.

Jessica slowly backed away from the table. She looked as if she were walking the plank on a ship.

"I wish I had my camera," Lila said. "I think this is going to go down in Sweet Valley Middle School history."

"Or at least in the yearbook," Mandy said, smiling at Lila and taking her camera out of her pocket.

Jessica furtively glanced around the lunchroom. She wanted to find the place where the fewest people she knew were sitting. Bruce Patman was on her left, so she turned right. There was Aaron—whoops. She turned around and found herself face-to-face with Peter.

It was no use hiding, Jessica decided. Everyone was going to hear her anyway. She wandered over a few tables, to the edge of the open section of the floor, and dropped down on one knee. She noticed a couple of people already staring at her, and she closed her eyes.

"Feelings," Jessica sang in a whisper. "Nothing more than feelings."

"Louder!" Mandy cried.

"We can't hear you!" Lila added.

Their shouts silenced the crowd.

"What are we trying to hear?" someone called out.

"Jessica's singing," Lila said. "It's a special Valentine's Day presentation."

Jessica opened one eye and scowled at Lila.

"Hit it, Jessica!" Bruce yelled.

Jessica gritted her teeth. "Feelings," she warbled. "Nothing more than feelings." She couldn't remember any of the other lyrics, so she started to improvise. "When you're around . . . I have a whole bunch of feeeeelings. . . ."

There were howls of laughter coming from all sides of the cafeteria. Jessica glanced at her watch. She still had a minute and a half to go.

"Trying to remember . . . all those feelings in my heart," Jessica continued, trying to remember the tune. "Feeeeeeelings. Whoa, whoa, whoa, feeelings," she burst out at the top of her lungs. "Whoa, whoa, whoa, feeeeelings . . ."

"Whoa, whoa! *Stop!*" Jerry yelled.

"You're killing us!" Julie cried, squealing with laughter.

"You're ruining my appetite," Danny shouted.

"Whoa, whoa, whoa, feeeelings . . ." Jessica looked at her watch again. Fifteen seconds left. "Nothing more than feeeeeeeelings. Feelings, feelings . . . lots of feelings, whoa, whoa." The second hand hit the twelve on her watch. "Whoa, whoa, whoa, the end." Jessica stood up, brushed the dust off her knees, and started to walk out of the lunchroom.

Suddenly everyone started clapping. People were standing onttheir chairs, applauding and cheering.

Jessica blushed and took a bow. She was just standing up again when she noticed Grace, sitting at the table right in front of her—and crying!

"Grace!" Jessica said, going over to her. "Come on, I know my singing isn't good, but is it *that* bad?" She sat down next to Grace and smiled.

Grace wiped her eyes with a napkin. "It's not that," she said. "I was upset before you started singing. That just made me feel worse."

"If it makes you feel any better, the song wasn't my idea," Jessica joked. "Believe me, it's not my idea of a good song. It's just that Mandy ordered me to do it—see, I'm her servant."

Grace nodded, sniffling a little. "I figured it was something like that."

"Why are you so sad?" Jessica asked. "Is there anything I can do?"

"I doubt it," Grace said. "It's Winston."

"Winston?" Jessica asked. "What do you mean?"

"'Feelings' is one of his favorite songs," Grace admitted, brushing off her eyelashes.

Jessica smiled. *That* figured.

"You know Winston and I are really good friends," Grace continued. "Actually, I like him a lot. But he and I had a huge fight last week about something really dumb, and we haven't made up yet. I'm still really upset about it."

Jessica nodded. It was hard to imagine anyone feeling romantic about Winston, but she supposed that everyone had the right to like whomever she wanted. And Grace had liked Winston for a while now.

Grace blew her nose into her napkin. "We were going to go to the dance together tomorrow night, only then we had that big fight, so I asked Peter Jeffries instead. I don't want to go with Peter—I want to go with Winston. But he won't even talk to me."

"That's great!" Jessica exclaimed, practically jumping out of her chair. "That's the best news I've had all day!"

"What? You think my fight with Winston is great?" Grace looked even more upset now. "Thanks a lot, Jessica. I know he's not as cool as Aaron, but he's a great guy and—"

"No!" Jessica waved her hands in the air to interrupt Grace. "You don't understand. See, I know someone who really likes Peter and wants to go to the dance with him. If I can get you and Winston back together, then Mandy can go with Peter. Right?" Jessica asked. "I mean, isn't that what you want?"

Grace nodded. "I'd be really happy if you could get Winston even to talk to me. And if he'd go to the dance with me, it would be fine if Mandy went with Peter. But I'm warning you—you shouldn't say anything to Mandy until you see what Winston says. Because getting us back together might just be impossible." She looked as if she might start crying all over again.

"It's not impossible," Jessica said confidently. This was the chance she'd been waiting for, the chance to make it all up to Mandy—and work a little Valentine's magic of her own. "Give me a piece of notebook paper. This is going to take a while for me to figure out."

"Do you really think you can do it?" Grace asked, sounding hopeful.

"Just trust me," Jessica said. "I have a good feeling about this."

"Elizabeth, that's not fair," Amy said.

"Who cares about fair? Was it fair when they dumped water on our heads instead of inviting us to the dance?" Elizabeth asked. "Was it fair when they changed the time on our watches last week, so we were late to class? Was it fair when they chained our bikes to that bench in the mall and hid the key?"

"No . . . but that was a long time ago," Amy argued. "They've changed since then."

"Maybe they changed their act, but *they* haven't changed," Elizabeth argued.

"I don't know," Julie said, looking at the invitations on the lunchroom table. "These *are* pretty nice."

"You guys! Are you blind?" Elizabeth demanded. "Just because Ken and Todd have been nice for the last twenty-four hours, and just because they sent us these dopey cards, doesn't mean they wouldn't do all that stuff to us again in a second if we let them."

"Elizabeth!" Amy cried. "It's Valentine's Day tomorrow. Do you know what that means? It means people start acting all weird about love. And that's what happened to Ken and Todd."

"No, that's what happened to you," Elizabeth teased her. "Come on. We have to stick to our plan. We're not done yet. They're only our servants for a few more hours. Don't you want to get your money's worth?"

"Well . . ." Amy seemed on the verge of giving in.

"It was hilarious in science class this morning," Julie said. "And I'll never forget the look on Mr. Clark's face when Todd crashed into him walking on his hands."

Amy grinned. "We are good, aren't we?"

"Phew." Elizabeth pretended to wipe sweat off her forehead. "You really had me worried there for a second. I thought you were going to go join the Unicorns on me, so you could talk about boys all the time."

"Shut up! I was not!" Amy cried, crumpling up her napkin and throwing it across the table at Elizabeth.

"So what's the next part of the plan?" Julie asked.

"Operation Embarrassment will continue at fourteen hundred hours," Elizabeth said. "That's two o'clock."

"I know that. But what are you going to do?" Julie asked.

"You'll have to wait and see," Elizabeth said.

Amy smiled. "Just like Ken and Todd."

"Have you noticed that Peter keeps looking over here?" Mary asked Mandy at the end of lunch period. "He's been staring at you for the lastttwo or three minutes."

"I bet he's sorry he asked Grace to the dance instead of you," Ellen said. "I bet he's totally regretting turning you down when you asked him yesterday."

"The important thing is, we got Jessica back for making Mandy go through that," Lila said.

Mandy shrugged. No matter what she told herself, she couldn't stop liking Peter. Even if he was taking Grace to the dance. Even if he didn't seem to like her back. "Was he really looking at me?" she asked Mary and Ellen.

Mary nodded. "Big time."

"I wonder what Jessica's talking to Grace about," Ellen said, peering across the lunchroom. "She's been over there for a long time."

"Singing lessons, probably," Lila joked.

Mandy smiled. Jessica's performance had been pretty funny. She felt a little guilty about making her suffer like that, but only a little. "And there's another Unicorn missing. Where is Janet today?" Mandy asked.

"Winston made her bring a picnic lunch and eat it with him," Lila said. "See them over there in the corner?" She pointed to where a red-and-white-checkered cloth was spread out on the floor.

"She must be dying!" Mandy said.

"Maybe, but I think it's pretty funny," Lila said. "I am *so* glad I didn't sign up to be anyone's servant!"

"Speaking of servants, what have you asked Peter to do today?" Mary asked.

"Is *that* why he keeps looking over here?" Mandy asked, horrified. "Because you told him to?"

"No!" Lila acted as if that were the silliest idea she had ever heard, when just yesterday she'd nearly ordered Peter to take Mandy to the dance. "I'd never do that. All I had him do today was clean out my locker. He did a really good job, too. I might hire him on a permanent basis."

"Lila!" Mandy cried.

"Just kidding." Lila smiled. "Wait—Jessica's coming this way." She waited until Jessica got a little closer, and then she called out, "Feelings! Whoa, whoa, whoa . . ."

Jessica glared at Lila and stuck out her tongue. Then she walked right past the table without saying a word.

Nine

◇

"Lloyd? Can I talk to you for a second?" Jessica asked in her sweetest, most innocent voice.

Lloyd looked up from his science magazine. "I'm right in the middle of a very interesting article."

"It'll only take a second, I promise." Jessica kneeled down beside him. "I need to ask you a favor."

Lloyd adjusted his glasses. "Did I hear you correctly? You want a favor from me?"

"I know, I'm not exactly on your list of favorite people right now. But this isn't to help me, really—it's to help two of my friends. You *did* say you believed in Valentine's Day when you agreed to switch with Aaron," Jessica reminded him.

"Well, er, yes. Something like that." Lloyd's ears turned bright red.

"So if I asked you to switch servants again, would that be OK?" Jessica asked. "All in the name of true love and Saint Valentine and all that."

"You mean . . . you want to be my servant again?" Lloyd asked.

"No!" Jessica said quickly. She had a feeling Lloyd was getting the wrong idea about her plan. "This doesn't involve me at all. Grace is your servant today, right?"

Lloyd nodded.

Jessica narrowed her eyes. "Hey, by the way, how come you're not making *her* do all that stuff you made me do?"

"Well, Jessica, to be perfectly candid, I—"

"Never mind," Jessica broke in. "I just want to know if Grace switched with someone else, if that would be OK with you."

"I suppose." Lloyd shrugged. "Who's the—"

"Great!" Jessica said, standing up. "That's all I needed to know. Thanks a lot, Lloyd. I'll send your new servant over right away."

"All right, but remember, you owe me a favor now," Lloyd said.

"Sure thing!" Jessica called over her shoulder as she hurried off to find Winston.

"There you are!" Jessica cried. "I've been looking all over for you." She leaned her hand against the brick wall opposite Winston's locker and tried to catch her breath.

"Is Lloyd making you run wind sprints now?" Winston joked.

Jessica shook her head. "Listen, I need to ask you a favor." She had to think of how she was going to sell this one. "I need you to switch servants with Lloyd today. Right away, actually."

"Is it that bad?" Winston patted Jessica's arm. "Don't worry, it'll get better when you two get to know each other a little more." He smiled at her.

He thinks I'm still Lloyd's servant! Jessica realized. *This might help.* "Oh, come on, Winston, please? Please let me trade and work for you instead. I'm sooo miserable."

"Well . . ." Winston tapped his finger against his chin. "I don't know. . . ."

"Hurry up and decide, will you?" Jessica asked impatiently.

"I guess I could—"

"Good. Then it's settled," Jessica said.

Winston grinned. "OK. Now get me a glass of water and bring it back here on your head."

Jessica shook her head. "I'm not your new servant."

"But we just traded," Winston said. "Didn't we?"

"You just switched servants with Lloyd," Jessica told him. "But I switched with Elizabeth yesterday, so I'm Mandy's servant, and now Grace is yours."

"Grace? No way," Winston grumbled. "Forget it."

"Winston, you agreed to switch!" Jessica said. "You promised."

Winston scratched his head. "I don't remember *promising*."

"And anyway, Grace wants to apologize to you for your argument last week. She's really sorry," Jessica told him.

"She is?" Winston suddenly looked hopeful.

"Uh-huh. And she wants to make up with you," Jessica said. "You know what else? She told me she wants to gotto the dance with you tomorrow night."

"Really? Are you serious?" Winston asked.

"Would *I* lie to you?" Jessica scoffed. "Come on. Let's find Grace. Then you can ask her to the dance." She took Winston's arm and started dragging him down the hall toward Grace's locker. They had only about two minutes before the lunch period was over.

"But I thought she was going with Peter Jeffries," Winston said.

"So she'll break the date," Jessica said with a shrug. "No big deal."

"But what if she says no?" Winston asked.

Jessica stopped walking and stared at him. "Winston, are you going to wimp out on me?

Because if you are—"

"No, I won't wimp out," Winston said.

"Good," Jessica said. "Anyway, even if Grace does say no, which she won't, she's your servant now—you can order her to go with you."

Winston suddenly stood up a little straighter. "You're right. I think I'm going to like this."

A minute later they approached Grace's locker. She looked shyly at Winston. "Hi."

"Hi," Winston said. "So . . . what's up?"

Jessica was standing behind Winston, and she hit him on the back. "Get on with it," she whispered.

"Right." Winston coughed. "Uh, Grace. I was wondering. Would you like to go to the Valentine's dance with me? I know you have to break your date with Peter, and I know I acted like a real jerk last week, and I'm sorry, but sometimes I just don't know what I'm saying and—"

"All right!" Grace cried. "Yes. The answer is yes."

"You mean it? You'll go to the dance with me?" Winston asked eagerly.

Grace nodded. "Of course I will, dummy."

The bell rang, and Jessica jumped into the air. "All right!" she cried.

Winston looked at her, a puzzled expression on his face. "You're *happy* we have to go to class now?"

"No, I'm happy that you guys are going to the dance together," Jessica said. "And pretty soon

Mandy's going to be happy, too!"

"What are you, Sweet Valley's own Cupid?" Winston joked as he and Grace walked down the hall toward social-studies class, side by side.

"What are you complaining about? It worked, didn't it?" Jessica shouted after him.

"Sure, but just wait until I tell Janet she's working for Lloyd now," Winston replied.

Jessica stopped walking. Janet? Working for Lloyd? *Uh-oh.*

"Boys! What on earth are you doing?" Mrs. Arnette turned around from the board and stared at Ken and Todd.

Ken looked up at her from underneath his desk. "It's really weird, but for some reason I can concentrate better down here," he told her.

Elizabeth looked at Amy and giggled.

"You know, it's been a seriously long time since this floor was cleaned," Todd said, wiping his finger along the floor and holding it up to show everyone the dust. "Probably not since 1952. Mrs. Arnette, you should take a look—there might be historical dust down here."

Everyone started laughing.

"Get back into your chairs this instant," Mrs. Arnette ordered, shaking her head. "I don't know what's gotten into everyone this week. You're all acting very strange. Now, as I was saying, the 1930s was the era of the Great Depression. . . ."

Elizabeth was taking notes when she heard a buzzing noise behind her.

"Zzzz . . ." Todd sat in his desk with his head back, snoring at the top of his lungs.

Ken kicked in with another loud snore; then he dropped his head onto his desk.

Mrs. Arnette walked over to their desks and clapped her hands together right in front of them. "Excuse me!" she said, sounding very frustrated.

"Huh?" Todd pretended to jerk awake and rubbed his eyes. "Mom, is that you?"

Everyone cracked up laughing again.

Mrs. Arnette shook her head and rapped Ken's desk with her knuckles.

Ken sat up and looked around with a startled expression on his face. "Did I fall asleep?"

"You most certainly did," Mrs. Arnette said. "Now, if you boys don't stop disrupting class, I'd be very happy to give you both detention slips. Would you like to spend your Friday afternoon in school?"

"Sorry," Todd said. "It won't happen again."

"Yeah, I'm really sorry," Ken said. "The last couple of days have been kind of rough."

"He's not kidding," Amy whispered to Elizabeth.

"I hope we don't get them in trouble," Elizabeth

said quietly.

"All right, then. We have only fifteen minutes of class time left," Mrs. Arnette said as she returned to the front of the classroom. "Let's try to get *something* accomplished."

"Lila, I think I have the whole thing figured out," Jessica said excitedly as she caught up with Lila in the hallway before her last class. "But I need your help. Can you come over to my house after school?"

Lila took a white crocheted sweater out of her locker and tied it around her shoulders. "What for?"

"For one thing, I want you to help me pick out what shoes and jewelry and stuff to wear tomorrow night for the dance," Jessica said, tossing her books into her locker. She stepped closer to Lila. "And, well, it's kind of a secret," she said in a low voice, "but I think I figured out how to get Peter to go to the dance with Mandy. See, I got Winston to trade with—"

Jessica felt a tap on her shoulder and turned around. Janet was standing behind her, looking furious. "Are you telling Lila about your fabulous *plan*?" she asked, tapping one foot against the floor.

Jessica smiled nervously. "I—"

"I guess it wasn't bad enough that I was Winston's servant—now I'm Lloyd's!" Janet practically yelled.

"What?" Lila looked amazed. "You're Lloyd's servant now?"

"I'm really sorry," Jessica said. "See, I was just trying to switch things around so Winston and—"

"Don't even try to make up some excuse. You did this on purpose," Janet said angrily.

"No, I didn't," Jessica said quickly. "I didn't even remember that you were Winston's servant until it was too late."

"Well, you're right—it *is* too late. Don't even bother apologizing," Janet said.

Jessica shrugged. "OK."

"Because somehow or other I'm going to get you back for this," Janet snapped. "I'm not about to spend the rest of my afternoon hanging out with Lloyd Benson!"

"But it's almost over," Lila said. "You won't have to do anything for him."

"Wrong," Janet said. "Lloyd has decided he's going to make me work all afternoon." She glared at Jessica. "But don't worry. I'll find some way to get out of it. And then you'll be the one who'll be sorry you made all these dumb switches!" Janet turned and stormed off down the hall.

"Jessica?" Lila asked. "As your best friend, I think I should warn you. You're in big trouble. Janet is really, really mad."

"Thanks for pointing that out," Jessica said sourly. She sighed as she walked down the hall toward her last class. *Why did I ever try to play matchmaker in the first place?*

"So that's the end of the master-servant project," Ken said with a sigh. "Too bad."

It was Friday afternoon, and he, Todd, Amy, and Elizabeth were walking home from school.

"Are you joking?" Elizabeth asked him.

"No," Ken said. "I really had a blast."

"Really?" Amy asked.

"Yeah," Todd said. "It's been so much fun. We got to do all this stuff I've always wanted to do—and we couldn't really get in trouble because we were just following orders."

Elizabeth hadn't really thought of it that way before. Maybe they really had enjoyed it. "Hey, can we buy you guys an ice-cream sundae or something, for being such good sports?" she asked.

"Yeah, come to Casey's with us," Amy said. "We'll buy you anything you want."

"That sounds great," Todd said. "But we're kind of busy this afternoon."

"Yeah, we have to get a bunch of stuff for the dance tomorrow," Ken said.

"What, are you renting tuxedos?" Amy joked. "This isn't the prom, you know."

"Oh, we know. It's just that we want to make the dance really special for you guys," Todd said.

"Yeah, it's going to be a great night," Ken added. "We'd better get going, so we can get everything we need. See you guys tomorrow!"

Elizabeth stared after Ken and Todd as they rode away on their bikes in the direction of the mall. "What happened to them?" she asked Amy.

"I don't know, but I like it," Amy said. "It sounds like they're going to buy us Valentine's presents!"

"Maybe we should get them something too," Elizabeth said. "Let's go to that sports store over on Grove Street." They walked toward the bike rack where their bicycles were locked.

"Tomorrow night is going to be so much fun!" Amy said. "Now that Todd and Ken have stopped acting so obnoxious to us, I bet we're going to have the best time."

"I know," Elizabeth said, unlocking her bike.

It was hard to believe, but Todd really was being kind of romantic. It felt kind of nice, having such a devoted Valentine. Weird, but nice.

Ten

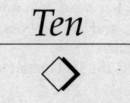

"We have to hurry, because your power as a master runs out soon," Jessica said, taking the steps up to her room two at a time.

"Didn't it already run out?" Lila asked, following her.

Jessica moved the hall phone into her room and closed the door behind them. She threw some stuff off the bed onto the floor, making room for the phone. "Not technically," she said. "As Lloyd told me, it never said anywhere on our signs and posters that the thing ended at the end of the school day. Since it's still Friday, you're still Peter's boss."

Lila sighed and sat down on the bed. She pulled out a pair of dirty socks from beneath her leg, made a face, and dropped them onto the floor. "OK, so what do you want me to do?"

"I have it from a very knowledgeable source that Grace decided to go to the dance with Winston instead of Peter," Jessica told Lila smugly.

"You're kidding!" Lila said.

Jessica shook her head. "So now all you have to do is call Peter, and as his boss, tell him to take Mandy to the dance."

Lila smoothed the bedspread with her hand. "I don't know."

"What do you mean, you don't know?" Jessica demanded. "Do you know how much work I had to do just to get to this point? You can't say no!"

"Well, in the first place, Mandy doesn't want me to order him around. I already offered to, and she said no," Lila told Jessica.

"Yeah, but you also know that she's dying to go with him, *and* she doesn't have another date yet," Jessica said. "And Peter doesn't have a date now, eithe~."

"True," Lila agreed. "But you know, you really humiliated Mandy the other day. I don't know why I should help *you*."

"Because I'm trying to help Mandy!" Jessica pleaded.

"Well . . ." Lila examined her nails for a minute. "OK, I'll do it."

"I'll dial," Jessica offered, handing Lila the phone, with her hand poised above the numbers.

"Not so fast," Lila said. "I have a couple of conditions."

"Conditions?" Jessica asked. "What do you mean?"

"I mean, I'll do it on three conditions," Lila said. "One, you have to do my math homework all next week."

"Lila!" Jessica protested. "That's not fair. Anyway, you know I'm not that good at math."

"Two," Lila continued, ignoring Jessica's objections, "you have to clean my room next week, too."

"Don't you have three maids to do that?" Jessica asked.

"*And*, three, you have to give me a complete manicure before the dance tomorrow," Lila said. "My nails look absolutely horrible." She held out one hand to demonstrate.

Jessica grabbed the phone back from her. "Forget it—I'll do it myself!" She glanced at Peter's number in the phone book and dialed.

"Hi, Peter," Jessica said. "This is Jessica Wakefield. I know it's kind of late to be asking you this, but do you already have a date for the Valentine's dance tomorrow?"

"I thought you were going with Aaron," Peter said. "Aren't you?"

"Oh, yeah," Jessica said. "I'm just asking . . . for a friend."

"Well, actually, I just had a big change of plans,"

Peter said. "But the answer is yes, I do have a date."

"Really?" Jessica's heart sank. How could he already have another date? He'd been dateless for only a couple of hours! "Well . . . um . . . can I ask who it is?"

"Mandy Miller," Peter said.

"What!" Jessica leaped into the air. "That's great! That's fantastic! That's stupendous! Thanks. I mean, it's too bad for my friend, she'll be very disappointed, but—anyway, I'll see you later."

"'Bye, Jessica," Peter said, sounding totally confused.

"Mandy's going with Peter!" Jessica cried, hanging up the phone. "Isn't that fantastic? And it's all because of me!"

Lila looked at her skeptically. "I don't think it's *all* because of you."

Jessica grinned. She knew Lila couldn't stand it when she was right.

The telephone rang, and Jessica grabbed it before it could ring twice. "Hello?" she said.

"Jessica! Guess what?" Mandy cried.

Mandy was talking so loud, Jessica had to hold the phone farther away from her ear. "What?" she asked.

"Peter asked me to the dance!" Mandy yelled. "Isn't that unbelievable?"

"Uh . . . yeah," Jessica said. Then she remembered she was supposed to be surprised by the news. "I mean, it's great! It's awesome! Tell me all about it. How did it happen? When did it happen?"

"Right after school," Mandy said excitedly. "Peter was *waiting* for me outside, can you believe it? He said that Grace had broken their date to go with Winston, and how he was glad, because he had wanted to go with me in the first place."

"He *did*?" Jessica asked. "That's so great!"

"Yeah. Only Grace asked him before he could ask me, and he felt kind of embarrassed, so he said yes," Mandy explained. "I guess Grace was having a fight with Winston, and she only asked Peter to try to make Winston mad."

"Wow. No kidding," Jessica said, smiling at Lila. "I didn't realize how complicated this was."

"Me either," Mandy said. "It seems like there are all these new couples at school. I guess it's because of Valentine's Day."

"I guess," Jessica said. "Unbelievable. Now you and Peter are one of them."

"I still can't believe it," Mandy said. "And you know what? Even if what you asked me to do seemed really terrible at the time, it actually *helped*. Peter said that he'd liked me for a while, only he was afraid to ask me out because he didn't know if *I* liked *him*. Then when I asked him to go, he figured out I liked him, too."

"That's incredible," Jessica said. "So what are

you going to wear to the dance? Do you have a funky outfit picked out already?"

"I don't know what I'm going to wear. Maybe you can come over tomorrow morning and help me pick something out," Mandy said. "But, Jessica, do you know what you did? Because you forced me to ask him, you helped me get together with Peter. So instead of being mad at you, I should have thanked you. So, thanks. And I'm sorry I made you sing that song."

"Oh, that's OK," Jessica said. "It was nothing."

Jessica smiled to herself as she hung up the phone. Mandy didn't need to know what really happened. The important thing was that Peter liked her and she liked him.

Maybe, just maybe, this Valentine's Day really was going to turn out all right.

After Mandy hung up the phone with Jessica, she wandered over to her closet and started searching through it for a dress to wear to the dance. She was most of the way through, and she still hadn't found anything she liked, when there was a knock on the door.

"Come in," Mandy called.

It was her mom. "Someone just dropped this off for you," Mrs. Miller said. "It was slipped under the door, and when I opened the door, there was nobody there." She handed an envelope to Mandy.

Mandy tore it open. Inside was an adorable Valentine's card, with a picture of a bulldog and a kitten dancing together. "Stranger things have happened on Valentine's Day," it said. The card was signed by Peter.

"Is it from a secret admirer?" her mother asked.

"Not anymore," Mandy said, smiling. "Mom, listen, I know I already spent my birthday money, but do you think we could go shopping tomorrow? I would *love* to get a new dress for the dance."

"Sure," Mrs. Miller said, wrapping her arm around Mandy's shoulders. "This guy must be pretty special, whoever he is."

Mandy sighed. "Definitely."

Saturday morning Elizabeth was wrapping the baseball cap she'd gotten for Todd when Steven yelled up the stairs, "Elizabeth! Phone!" Elizabeth put down the spool of ribbon and went into the hall.

"Hello?" she said.

"Hi, Elizabeth, it's Todd. What's up?"

"Oh . . . nothing much," Elizabeth said. "What's up with you?"

"Well, my dad's about to take me to the flower shop so I can pick up a corsage for you," Todd said.

Elizabeth practically dropped the phone. "A corsage?"

"Yeah. Ken and I thought of it yesterday, when we were shopping," Todd said.

Ken and Todd, shopping together? It was hard to picture. Usually when Elizabeth went to the mall with them, they went off to play video games. "That's really nice," Elizabeth said.

"So my dad said I should ask what color dress you're wearing, so it'll match," Todd said.

"Oh. Well, I think I'm wearing blue," Elizabeth said. "So I guess white would be good. Or maybe pink."

"Pink sounds better—it's Valentine's Day, right?" Todd asked. "Which reminds me, happy Valentine's Day."

"Thanks," Elizabeth said. "Same to you." For a second she didn't know who she was talking to. Was that really Todd, deciding on pink because it was Valentine's Day?

"OK, I'd better get going. Ken and I will pick you and Amy up around seven, is that OK? My dad offered to drive if your parents will pick us up," Todd said.

"OK, I'll ask them," Elizabeth said. "I'm sure it'll be fine."

"Great," Todd said. "I'm really looking forward to it. See you later!"

Elizabeth just stared at the telephone for a minute after she had hung up. Todd was really looking forward to their date, *and* he'd bought her a corsage? Elizabeth felt her stomach flutter. She felt nervous, happy, and excited, all at the same time. She couldn't help it. She was getting as mushy as Amy.

She decided to call Amy, to try to talk herself out of it.

"I was just about to call you!" Amy said when she picked uptthe phone. "You are *not* going to believe this. Ken just told me he's bringing me a corsage tonight."

"I know—I mean, so is Todd," Elizabeth told her. "He even wanted to make sure it would match my dress. Can you believe that? Isn't there something wrong with this picture?"

"Elizabeth, stop being so suspicious! It's Valentine's Day. They're trying to make up for all the rotten things they did," Amy insisted.

"I guess," Elizabeth said. "Maybe they really are being sincere. They seem really excited aboutthe dance. Todd even arranged our ride already. Usually he leaves it to the last minute."

"Last time Ken and I went to a dance, he told me to ride my bike and meet him there!" Amy said. "But you know what? Ken said he's bringing me a present, too. Isn't he the sweetest?" she asked in a dreamy voice.

"But, Amy? Don't get too carried away," Elizabeth said.

"Why not? It's Valentine's Day!" Amy said. "That's what it's for, right?"

Elizabeth laughed. "I guess you're right."

Amy sighed. "I think this dance is going to be something we'll always remember."

Eleven

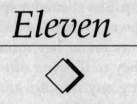

"Pass the hair spray!" Ellen yelled from the bathroom between Elizabeth's and Jessica's bedrooms. Several of the Unicorns had come to Jessica's house to get ready for the dance.

Jessica lobbed the bottle of hair spray through the air, and Ellen caught it. "Hurry up in there, I still need to put on my makeup!" Jessica called to her.

"You're not even dressed yet!" Ellen replied.

Jessica was still ironing her new purple-flowered dress, which had somehow gotten trampled in her room before she'd even had a chance to hang it up.

"Hi, guys," Mandy said, walking into the room. Her hair was pulled back in a loose French braid, and she was wearing a gorgeous pink strapless dress.

"I love your dress!" Mary said. "Where did you get it?"

"Believe it or not, it's straight from the Attic," Mandy said proudly. The Attic was Mandy's favorite thrift shop. She cleared a space on the bed so she could sit down. "Where's Elizabeth?"

"She and Amy areiin her room, getting ready," Grace said. "They're flipping out because Ken and Todd are coming any minute, and they're supposedly bringing corsages."

"Corsages? Really?" Tamara Chase said. She leaned closer to the small mirror above Jessica's dresser and put on a fresh coat of pink lipstick. "I guess Todd and Ken are more mature than I thought."

"Hey, Mandy, I've been meaning to ask you. How much money did we end up making for the hospital?" Mary asked.

"About eight hundred dollars," Mandy said. "Isn't that incredible?"

"That's awesome!" Mary said.

"No offense, Mandy, but I am *so* glad that whole master-servant thing is over with," Jessica said, putting the finishing touches on her dress. "I mean, it's great that we earned so much money. But what a mess."

"Yeah, but how about Janet getting stuck with Winston and Lloyd?" Mandy said. "That was pretty hilarious, wasn't it?"

* * *

"How do I look?" Elizabeth fastened the silver barrette in her hair and stood in front of Amy.

"Perfect," Amy said. She glanced at her watch. "They're going to be here any minute. I'm so nervous!"

"Me too," Elizabeth said. "But why? I mean, I hang out with Todd practically every day. We've been to dances before, too."

"Yeah, but not like *this* one," Amy said. "It seems like we're all so much more grown-up this time." She started brushing her hair again.

"Amy, if you brush your hair any more, you're not going to have any left," Elizabeth said.

"Sorry. I just want to make sure I look good when Ken sees me." Amy set the brush back down on Elizabeth's bureau.

"Just relax. You look great," Elizabeth told her.

Suddenly they heard the doorbell. "Elizabeth! Amy! Todd and Ken are here," Mr. Wakefield yelled up the stairs a minute later.

Amy nervously spritzed her hair with styling gel one more time before running out the door. "OK, here goes nothing."

"Look what Aaron gave me! Isn't it beautiful?" Jessica held the red rose to her nose and sniffed.

"Not as beautiful as the locket Tim gave me,"

Lila teased. She held out the silver necklace to show Jessica.

"Can you believe Mandy and Peter are *still* dancing together?" Belinda asked, shaking her head. "I think they're in love." She tugged at the string of a red heart-shaped helium balloon that was floating pavt them. "The decorations look great, don't they?"

"You wouldn't be in charge of the decorations committee, would you?" Lila teased her.

"Well, maybe," Belinda said. "See all those pink Cupids made out of construction paper on the wall over there? I made those."

Jessica dipped the ladle into the punch bowl and served glasses of the cherry punch to her friends. "Hey, Lila, did Mandy tell you how much we made for the hospital?"

"Something like eight hundred dollars," Lila said. "If you count what people's parents added to what we raised. Daddy would give more, but he already donated a whole wing to the hospital, and he didn't want to overdo it."

Jessica looked at Belinda and shook her head. Lila took every opportunity she could to brag about how rich she was.

"Here comes Janet," Lila said. "Maybe you'd better hide, Jessica."

"I'm not worried," Jessica said. "I mean, she

can't kill me in a public place, right?" She smiled nervously.

"How's it going, Janet?" Belinda asked.

"Great," Janet said in a cheerful voice. "For once they're actually playing decent music."

Janet loves compliments. Compliment her and maybe she won't be so mad, Jessica thought. "You're such a great dancer, Janet. And I like your dress," she said. "It looks great on you."

"Thanks, Jessica." Janet helped herself to some punch. "I like your dress, too."

Jessica practically fell over. The last thing she expected was for Janet to compliment her back.

"Hey, how did it go with Lloyd yesterday?" Belinda asked. "Not to bring up a touchy subject or anything."

Jessica frowned. Did Belinda *have* to remind Janet of that now, just when she seemed to be in a good mood? She waited for Janet to go off on some tirade about how horrible Jessica was.

Instead Janet just smiled. "Oh, it was OK. Actually, he didn't make me do much at all."

Jessica looked out onto the dance floor, where Lloyd was standing with Leslie Forsythe. "He didn't make you do anything?" she asked Janet. "That's nice."

"Well, I'd better get back to Denny before he misses me," Janet said. "See you guys!"

"Wow, she's not even mad at you anymore," Lila said.

"Must be the Valentine Effect," Belinda said.

"The Valentine Effect?" Jessica asked.

"Yeah, it makes weird people act normal and normal people act weird. Jim actually gave me one of those heart-shaped boxes of chocolates," Belinda said. "I think he's losing his mind."

"Well, whatever makes Janet act normal is OK with me," Jessica said, feeling relieved. Was it possible that she really was off the hook?

"Thanks for the presents—they're great," Todd said, putting the Dodgers cap backward on his head. It looked a little funny with his jacket and tie, but Elizabeth couldn't help thinking he looked pretty cute anyway. "We have some for you, too."

Amy looked at Elizabeth and grinned. So far the dance was going really well. Elizabeth loved her corsage—it was made of tiny pink roses and baby's breath, and looked beautiful with her dress.

"Here you go." Ken handed Amy a small gift wrapped in red tissue paper. "Happy Valentine's Day. I hope you like it."

"I'm sure I'll love it," Amy said, tearing off the paper. "Ah—ahhhchooo!"

"Bless you," Elizabeth said.

"Excuse me," Amy said, wiping her nose with a

tissue. "Boy, I wonder if I'm allergic to something in here. That must be thettenth time I've sneezed since we got here."

"The gym's kind of dusty," Todd said.

Amy took off the last piece of tape and uncovered a small square box. She slowly lifted the top off the box. Inside was a tiny pair of earrings, in the shape of hearts. "Thanks, Ken—I love them. They're beau—ahhhhchoooo!" Amy looked up at him and smiled sheepishly. "Excuse me," she said in a very nasal voice. "They're beautiful."

Todd handed a box to Elizabeth. "This is kind of boring, but it was all I could think of."

Elizabeth unwrapped the large, heart-shaped box of chocolates. "No, it's not. It's great," she said, opening the box. "I love chocolates. Even the ones with pink goo inside. Here, have one." She smiled at Todd and he smiled back.

I shouldn't have been so suspicious of Todd, she thought. This was turning out to be the most wonderful Valentine's Day.

"Let's dance," Todd suggested, taking Elizabeth's hand. "I love this song."

"Me too—" Elizabeth came to a halt and covered her nose with her hand. "Ahhhhhchooo!"

"Maybe we should take a break," Mandy said. "My feet are getting kind of tired."

"Good idea." Peter took Mandy's hand, and they walked over to the punch bowl.

I can't believe he's holding my hand! Mandy thought, feeling a flutter of excitement in her stomach. The night was going even better than she'd hoped. The most surprising thing of all was that she didn't feel nervous around Peter anymore. They'd spent practically the whole evening together, talking and laughing.

She'd told him what it was like growing up without a dad, and he'd told her how he and his stepmother didn't always get along. And she'd found out that Peter wasn't quite as perfect as she'd thought—he'd stepped on her toes about eight times during a slow dance. He wasn't embarrassed, though. They had just made up a new dance that included stepping on each other's toes, until they were laughing so hard they had to stop dancing.

Peter poured two cups of the cherry punch and handed one to Mandy. "This is a pretty good dance, considering it's at school," he said.

Mandy laughed. "I know. I think they decided to hire a real DJ instead of asking Mr. Clark to pick out the music this time."

Peter started laughing. "You must be right. I haven't heard 'Feelings' once."

"Hi!" Jessica said, coming up to both ofthem.

"Are you having fun?" Aaron was right behind her.

"Jessica, we were just talking about you," Peter said.

"You were? Why?" Jessica asked.

"We were talking about your favorite song. You know, the one you sang in the lunchroom yesterday with so much feeeeling," Peter said.

"And it was a good thing I did, too," Jessica said.

"*Why?*" Aaron laughed.

"Oh . . . never mind," Jessica said. "I'm just glad Mandy was my boss for only one day, instead of two."

"So am I," Mandy said.

Jessica nudged Mandy in the ribs once the boys got involved in a conversation. "So how's it going?" she whispered.

"Perfect," Mandy said. "Thanks again."

"Oh, no problem," Jessica said. "Just call me Cupid."

Twelve

◇

"Ahh—ahhh—ahhchooo!"

Amy blew her nose again, which was turning red from so much sneezing. "I can't believe we're both coming down with colds on the night of the Valentine's dance," she complained. "Talk about lousy timing."

She and Elizabeth were standing in the girls' bathroom, fixing their hair, about halfway through the dance.

"Ahhhchoooo!" Elizabeth covered her nose with a tissue. "It's hard to dance the way we've been sneezing." She put on some more lip gloss, then grabbed a tissue just before she sneezed again.

"No kidding," Amy said, adjusting the back on one of her new earrings. "Do you think we might actually be allergic to something in the gym? Maybe it's Lila's obnoxious perfume."

"Yeah, maybe, but she's not in here," Elizabeth pointed out as Amy sneezed again.

"Then what is it? It's not like I'm wearing anything new. I used the same shampoo. I didn't even feel sick until Ken came to pick us up," Amy said.

"It doesn't really feel like a cold," Elizabeth said. "I don't have any other symptoms."

Amy smacked her fist against the sink. "This is so frustrating! Everything was going so perfectly!"

"I know," Elizabeth said sadly. "Todd and Ken are being so incredibly sweet. They gave us gifts, they brought us corsages. And we can't even carry on a conversation because we keep sneezing." She bent down and sniffed her corsage.

"Ahhhchooo! Ahhhchooo! Ahhhchooo!"

"Elizabeth, are you OK?"

Elizabeth blew her nose and tried to catch her breath. "Hey, Aby, cad you do me a favor? Sbell your corsage."

Amy looked at her in bafflement. "Sure, OK." She bent down and sniffed the cluster of tiny yellow roses.

"Ahh—ahh—ahh-choooo! Ahhchooo!"

When Amy recovered from her sneezing fit, she stared at Elizabeth, her eyes widening in disbelief.

"Are you thinking what I'm thinking?" Elizabeth asked grimly.

Amy nodded.

They both unpinned their corsages and dropped them into the toilet. Plunk! Plunk!

"Sneezing powder," they both said at the same time.

"I had such a great time," Jessica told Aaron after they had danced the last dance, a slow Johnny Buck song that was one of Jessica's favorites. "You're the best Valentine."

"So are you," Aaron said, looking down at his feet.

"My mom should be here pretty soon," Jessica said.

"Want to go wait outside?" Aaron asked.

"That sounds great," Jessica said. "But I have to hang around here for a couple more minutes, OK?"

"Why?" Aaron asked.

"You'll see. Come on, let's see if there're any of those little candy hearts left." Jessica put her arm through Aaron's. They walked over to the refreshment table.

"Hey, there's Ken. I have to ask him something, I'll be back in a second," Aaron promised.

"OK," Jessica said, walking over to the table by herself. She was just about to reach into the bowl of pastel hearts when she felt someone tugging on the sleeve of her dress. She turned and saw Lloyd standing next to her. "Hi, Lloyd," she said cheerfully. "What's up?" She took a few hearts out of the bowl and tossed one into her mouth. Even talking to Lloyd couldn't ruin the fun night she'd had.

"This is what is up." Lloyd handed Jessica a piece of paper.

I hope it's not a valentine, Jessica thought, feeling panicky. She skimmed the official-looking paper. "What?" she cried. "What is this?"

"It's a certificate guaranteeing me one more afternoon of servant duty," Lloyd said calmly. "Provided by you."

"Me? Why me?" Jessica looked at the paper again. It said: *An afternoon of servitude provided by the Unicorn of Your Choice.* Someone had written her name on that line.

"I don't know, exactly," Lloyd said. He shook his head and his glasses slipped down his nose. "Janet made out this certificate. She's the one who authorized it."

"But the master-servant thing is over already," Jessica pleaded. "How can I owe you an afternoon?"

"Janet wasn't feeling well yesterday. She gave me this as a rain check," Lloyd said, taking back the certificate.

"She looked fine to me," Jessica muttered.

"Now, don't worry—I won't keep you busy all afternoon," Lloyd assured her. "Only three or four hours. I'm working on a critical chemistry experiment."

"Three or four hours? On a Sunday?" Jessica stood there, stunned.

"I'll call you in the morning," Lloyd said. "Happy Valentine's Day!"

Jessica crumbled the one candy heart left in her hand. So much for a beautiful evening.

The DJ tapped his fingers against the microphone. "May I have your attention, please. I bet you all thought the night was over—but don't put your coats on yet!"

A lot of people who were heading to the door stopped and turned around.

"I have a very special treat for you this evening," the DJ said. "I understand we have two aspiring rock and rollers in the building."

Elizabeth giggled and clutched Amy's arm.

"Ken Matthews and Todd Wilkins, will you please come up to the table here?"

Elizabeth glanced over at Ken and Todd, who were standing with a group of their friends.

"What for?" Ken asked.

"We have a special request from the audience," the DJ said. Elizabeth, Amy, Mandy, Belinda, and Jessica started yelling and cheering.

"Go, Todd!" Elizabeth cried.

"They'd like you to sing one of their favorite songs. I understand it's a very popular one around school this week. Would you please come up here, boys? I want to make sure everyone hears you," the DJ said.

Bruce, Aaron, and Charlie pushed Todd and Ken up to the DJ's table. Their faces were bright red, and they were dragging their feet. Everyone gathered around in a circle, and Belinda and Julie started to chant, "Go Todd! Go Ken! Go Todd! Go Ken!" Other kids joined in, shouting their names.

"Stand here, please," the DJ said, gesturing for Ken and Todd to get up onto two chairs. "I'll hand you the microphone, and you two just jump in when you feel ready." He cued a CD, and the opening notes of "Feelings" boomed out into the gym.

"Go Todd! Go Ken!" everyone yelled.

Ken was looking out at the crowd, a horrified expression on his face. Todd stared straight down at his feet.

"OK, take it from the top!" the DJ cried, handing the microphone to Todd.

"Janet! How could you do that to me?" Jessica leaned into the Fowlers' car window. Janet and Lila were getting a ride home together in Lila's father's limousine.

"Do what?" Janet asked innocently.

"By the way—Jess, Ken and Todd did a *much* better job than you," Lila said, laughing.

"They had a nice harmony, didn't they?" Janet commented.

"I'm talking about that stupid phony certificate you gave Lloyd," Jessica said, staring angrily at Janet.

"Oh, that. Well, you know, I wasn't feeling well yesterday afternoon," Janet said.

"Right," Jessica said. "You were very sick. So sick that Elizabeth just told me she bumped into you when you were shopping yesterday!"

"Sometimes shopping makes me feel better. What can I say? I guess I just made a speedy recovery." Janet gave Jessica a superior look. "Have fun with Lloyd tomorrow."

"But it's not fair," Jessica argued. "The master-servant thing is over, and I was already a servant for two whole days. Besides, you know how much Lloyd likes to make me work."

"I know." Janet smiled. "I think he said something about planning an outdoor experiment. Something about collecting bugs and spiders and putting them on slides."

"We gotta go," Lila said. "Have fun with Lloyd tomorrow. The rest of us are going to see *The Bogeyman, Part Twelve* at the mall."

"But it's not fair!" Jessica cried.

"Don't worry—we'll tell you all about it," Lila said. "Say hi to Lloyd for me."

"Janet!" Jessica said. "How could you do this?"

"It was nothing. You can thank me later." Janet pressed a button, and the window closed automatically, right in Jessica's face.

"Guess what? Peter asked me to go a movie next weekend," Mandy said happily.

It was Monday afternoon, and the Unicorns were piled into Mrs. Miller's minivan. They were going to Children's Hospital to deliver their donation and visit with the children in the cancer ward.

"It's only Monday," Lila said. "He asked you already?"

"What did you expect? He's in love," Belinda teased.

Mandy blushed.

"How was your date with Lloyd yesterday?" Mary asked Jessica.

Jessica folded her arms across her chest. "It wasn't a date. It was an afternoon at a scummy pond with the world's worst scientist."

"OK! OK!" Mary said, laughing. "Sorry I asked."

Mrs. Miller stopped at a stoplight and turned around to face them in the backseat. "I hope you girls are proud of yourselves. You really have done something amazing."

"It's an important cause," Mary said.

"Yeah," Jessica added. "And it was Mandy's idea. Which reminds me." She pulled a rolled-up piece of paper out of her pocket. "Lloyd wanted me to give this to you." She smiled.

"What is it?" Mandy asked, looking suspiciously at the piece of paper.

"You'll see," Jessica said.

Mandy unrolled the paper. "What does that mean?"

"I had to leave Lloyd a little early yesterday—family plans," Jessica said with a shrug. "And since this whole thing *was* your idea, I thought you could be Lloyd's servant for the last fifteen minutes of his contract. He crossed out my name and wrote yours in." She grinned at Mandy. "Have fun."

"What?" Mandy demanded.

"What's that saying about fifteen minutes of fame?" Lila asked.

"More like fifteen minutes of pain," Janet added.

Mandy threw the certificate back at Jessica. "No way!"

"Well, it *was* your great idea," Jessica teased. "It's only fair that you get to share Lloyd with me and Janet."

"Yeah, we wouldn't want to keep him *all* to ourselves," Janet said, laughing.

*   *   *

"Todd, you have more talent than I ever imagined," Elizabeth teased him on Monday afternoon. "Why don't you give up on basketball and become a lounge singer instead?" She had just gotten out of the *Sixers* office, where she was working on the next edition.

Todd shook his head. "Ha ha. Very funny." He tried to frown at Elizabeth, but he burst out laughing.

Elizabeth started laughing, too.

"Truce?" Todd asked.

"Truce," Elizabeth said.

He picked up her backpack and slung it over his shoulder. "Can I buy you a sundae at Casey's?" he asked.

"Oh, sure. Now what? A sundae with shaving cream instead of whipped cream? Aneexploding cherry?" Elizabeth asked, giggling. Suddenly she stopped outside of Mr. Bowman's office.

She pointed to a notice on his bulletin board. "Did you hear about this new creative-writing class Mr. Bowman's organizing?"

Todd groaned. "Another class? Don't we have enough?"

"This one's special," Elizabeth said. "It's only going to meet twice a week for four weeks, and it's going to be taught by a real writer."

"I bet you already signed up for it, right?" Todd asked.

Elizabeth shook her head. "You can't sign up—you have to get picked for it."

"I'm sure they'll pick you," Todd said.

Elizabeth smiled. "I hope they pick you, too."

Todd shook his head. "Actually, I hope they don't. It might get in the way of basketball practice."

"I'm sure the coach wouldn't mind if you missed a few practices," Elizabeth said.

A cloud seemedtto pass over Todd's face. "The coach might not mind, but my dad would. He doesn't want anything to get in the way of basketball."

What will happen when Todd discovers he has other interests besides basketball? Find out in Sweet Valley Twins and Friends #77, **TODD RUNS AWAY.**

SIGN UP FOR THE
SWEET VALLEY HIGH®
FAN CLUB!

Hey, girls! Get all the gossip on Sweet
Valley High's® most popular teenagers
when you join our fantastic Fan Club!
As a member, you'll get all of this really
cool stuff:

- Membership Card with your own
  personal Fan Club ID number
- A Sweet Valley High® Secret
  Treasure Box
- Sweet Valley High® Stationery
- Official Fan Club Pencil (for secret
  note writing!)
- Three Bookmarks
- A "Members Only" Door Hanger
- Two Skeins of J. & P. Coats® Embroidery
  Floss with flower barrette instruction
  leaflet
- Two editions of *The Oracle* newsletter
- Plus exclusive Sweet Valley High®
  product offers, special savings,
  contests, and much more!

Be the first to find out what Jessica & Elizabeth Wakefield are up to by joining the
Sweet Valley High® Fan Club for the one-year membership fee of only $6.25 each
for U.S. residents, $8.25 for Canadian residents (U.S. currency). Includes shipping
& handling.

Send a check or money order (do not send cash) made payable to "Sweet Valley
High® Fan Club" along with this form to:

SWEET VALLEY HIGH® FAN CLUB, BOX 3919-B, SCHAUMBURG, IL 60168-3919

NAME_____
            (Please print clearly)

ADDRESS_____

CITY_____ STATE _____ ZIP_____
                                                        (Required)

AGE _____ BIRTHDAY_____ /_____ /_____

Offer good while supplies last. Allow 6-8 weeks after check clearance for delivery. Addresses without ZIP
codes cannot be honored. Offer good in USA & Canada only. Void where prohibited by law.
©1993 by Francine Pascal   LCI-1383-123